CLAR

MW01705556

FICTION

The Miracle Lambs of Minane —*Finbarr O'Reilly*.................................... 1

Sparrow — *Yilin Wang*.. .19

When We Were Starless — *Simone Heller*.. 25

The Facecrafter — *Anna Wu*.. 54

Thirty-Three Percent Joe — *Suzanne Palmer*... 77

In Everlasting Wisdom — *Aliette de Bodard*.. 97

The Falls: A Luna Story — *Ian McDonald*... 112

NON-FICTION

Endless Forms Most Horrible: Parasites and SF — *Julie Novakova*... 129

First Contact, Fantasy, and Cooperation:
A Conversation with Steven Erikson — *Chris Urie*............................ 136

Another Word: In Praise of Taking it Slow — *Sarah Pinsker*............... 141

Editor's Desk: After the Dirty Dozen — *Neil Clarke*............................ 145

Postcards from Asia: The Floodplain (Cover Art) — *Pat Presley*...... 148

Neil Clarke: Publisher/Editor-in-Chief
Sean Wallace: Editor
Kate Baker: Non-Fiction Editor/Podcast Director

Clarkesworld Magazine (ISSN: 1937-7843) • Issue 145 • October 2018

www.clarkesworldmagazine.com

The Miracle Lambs of Minane

FINBARR O'REILLY

It was midsummer when I arrived in Corcaigh from Sadbhsfort, and the famine parties were in full swing.

I don't know if you remember the posters for them—in a vibrant shawl, a red-headed woman stands, holding a twin in each arm. Around her is a lush green and golden valley, and her back is to the distant ocean, its waters boiling with the mechanical monsters that had closed the seas and caused the famines.

Underneath, lettered in a white, art deco font: "The country needs people."

That much was true. You couldn't walk the city without crossing streets keening their loss through curtains flapping against broken glass, where little lived within the moldering papered walls but feral cats and rats, one feeding off the other.

The parties were the brainwave of a local Bishop. The generations following a famine usually produce more female children than male, they said, but in Corcaigh the problem was more severe and durable than in Dublin and Galway. The parties, correctly chaperoned, of course, allowed solid rural women to meet observant city boys. Apparently, what the country needed was the right kind of people.

More on the hunt for work than for love, I had been to a few such events, but it quickly became clear that the carbolic-scented men they attracted would struggle to score in a brothel, and the women were not to my taste. In any case, the ever-present chaperones meant any chance of a frolic was low. Hands above the table, nobody standing closer than a paperback's length apart, awkward conversation accompanied by bad, state-issued food. There is only so much turnip mash, potato cakes, or German noodles, basically potato by another name, that one can eat.

Having left one such evening about six weeks into my stay in the city, I bumped into a compatriot of mine, Creedon, who twisted my arm until I agreed to attend another party. We could always bribe a guard for breaking the curfew, there may even be work in it for me, it was on the way home, I was told, and sure to be good, as the chaperone, an American woman called Mrs. Weber, was "a friend."

We walked up from the river, past the burned-out ruins of the old art college, to a fine, yellow-fronted house just beyond the cathedral, buttery light gifting itself from every window.

We were in the door ten minutes, bramble gin in hand, when Maura Verane made her entrance.

A short woman with a tanned, lined face and untamed hair the color of a slumbering coal fire, her "coatigan"—a vast garment composed of differently sized mohair panels, one more garishly colored than its neighbor—flapped about her, snagging on chairbacks as she waded through kisses and handshakes. None of this attention moved her to smile.

"Can you believe that one is a farmer," said Creedon, who professed to know Moll and told me she was something of a celebrity around the city.

"She was one of the first to stop growing potatoes and turnips. She was a bigwig in the university and as soon as the worst of the emergency was over, she started growing herbs—dill and basil and the like. Now she supplies fruit and veg to the best restaurants, the best houses, the Bishops. Sure, they're only throwing money at her."

Moll circled the room as she deposited jewels—chilies, tomatoes, yellow bell peppers so perfect they looked injection-molded—on the large dining table. We had enough calories by then, of course, if never quite enough booze, but Moll brought something of the spice and color of the pre-famine years to a crowd not quite wealthy or powerful enough to acquire it themselves, and they loved her for it.

As a coda to her entrance and a signal that she had blessed the dinner to indeed start, Moll finished with something special.

Creedon was fizzing with excitement: "Once, she brought lemons."

Moll's finale was a corker. She reached into the deep breast pocket of her vast woolens and hefted in her talons a heavy bottle of oil, its contents shining through the thick glass walls as if squeezed from sunlight itself.

"From our Sicilian friends at the golf course," she announced, holding it up for all to see. God knows what it cost her.

"The Sicilians" was how almost everybody in Corcaigh referred to the Mediterranean refugees, regardless of their actual nationalities.

Driven from their homes by the migration north of murderous African summers, they had settled in the hills and largely deserted suburbs to the south of the city, colonizing the parched golf courses of Douglas and Mahon with olive groves and citrus trees.

Moll's performance over, we sat, the few elders at the tables, the rest of us cross-legged on the floor or perched on the piano or a sofa's arm, and we talked and ate for pleasure rather than mere survival.

I first tasted a tomato that night. The flesh had an earthly perfume, but it was the skin that amazed me most, the texture of something so slick on one side and so rough on the other, parting with a click when I could maneuver it between my teeth.

So it was that I was trying to unstick a large piece of tomato skin from an incisor when Creedon guided Moll to stand in front of me, raising eyebrows to one or the other of us as if to say "This is who I told you about."

Moll looked me up and down and said, "so I hear you're looking for a job?"

Like a fool, I kept my mouth shut and nodded.

Moll's "farm," on the hills above Minane Bridge, was one-and-a-half acres of raised beds, with plants and herbs of every color and shape, plus about eight acres of grazing land, a smattering of large greenhouses, and a dozen polytunnels. A few goats gave milk and she kept hens for eggs.

The farm had probably been there in some form during the "Great" Famine, more than two centuries earlier.

Some of the farmhouse walls were stone, some badly mortared rubble, and a few just rammed earth sloshed with whitewash, but it was dry and it was solid. The structure was split in two—Moll lived in the main part of the house, surrounded by overstuffed furniture upholstered in embroidered silk, a curious combination for a woman with such a reputation for a hard edge. A one-room section at the northern end was mine, with a window, a fireplace, a kitchen table, and a low bed hidden behind a curtain.

Across the courtyard were a couple of long-empty milking sheds, crammed with troughs, flowerpots in resilient clay and crumbling plastic, and farm and garden implements that looked like they were drawn from a dozen cultures and as many centuries. Harrows so old the wood had petrified to near stone lay interlocked with spiral ploughs in shining stainless steel and a collection of corroding scythes and sickles, in a teetering, tetanus-riddled puzzle.

Sniffing the rust in the air, I wondered how much of this kelter had been assembled before the famine, how many of these implements had been hauled and swung and driven by one of Moll's ancestors, and when I would get to use them.

I needn't have bothered—for the first three months of my "apprenticeship," I was weeding, or mixing "nettle tea" to feed the plants, or moving barrows of fertilizer, dug from three large mounds of manure and human excrement buried in the east field.

After that, I graduated to harvesting. This mostly consisted of pushing a battered shopping trolley of equipment up and down the paved lanes of Maura's raised beds and grow houses while she barked instructions at me.

"Basil, mint, lettuce—tear them. Chives, dill, rocket—cut."

If her work was done and the evening was mild, she would sometimes break off from instruction or admonishment, sit on a bucket, and reminisce.

"A long time before the famines," she once told me, "my grandfather lived in a fishing village further down the coast. When he was a boy, if times were tough, his mother would cook lobster for them. In those days, fishermen would give them away on the quays—they were unsellable sea vermin, but they were the only protein a lot of families had.

"So he said she would boil them up and then dribble a precious little bit of melted butter and a bit of wild garlic over the top. Very tasty, he said they were.

"But then, after the family had eaten, his mother would have him bury the shells in the back garden rather than put them out in the rubbish, for fear the neighbors or the binmen would see how poor they were.

"Years later, by the time my mother was a young woman, my grandfather was a prosperous man in printing in the city and the family ate out in restaurants—Greens and the like—and lobster had enjoyed something of a re-branding. If it was on the menu, my grandfather would laugh his head off at all the nobs paying through the nose for something his mother found as shameful as eating rats. He never ordered it, though."

Below the farm, in the village, a phone line ran to Tom Buckley's bar. Tom's surviving grandmother, apart from helping Moll out with harvesting or canning, took calls on her behalf from clients in the city. Four mornings a week, I would do the rounds of the lean-to's and polytunnels, snipping and tearing, until my orders and my panniers were filled.

Before nine, I would set off. Moll had gifted me a bicycle, which, by its weight, must have been made of meteoric iron, and by its age, her grandfather had forged.

Around the city, I quickly became known as "the Rocket"—with Corkonian efficiency in piss-taking, this referred to my cargo as much as my limited uphill speed.

Corcaigh sits in a drained marsh at the bottom of a cloud-topped bowl of hills, so there were inclines to be conquered on any route from Minane and back again.

The safest route ran alongside the fence of the old airport, by that time mostly given over to rescue 'copters and lumbering cargo aerostats. Sadly, it was also the biggest hill and Moll's antique bike would develop a precarious wobble as I crested it, straining myself out of the saddle to make anything faster than walking pace.

I was always careful with my cargo—it was worth a lot. But I was not so careful that I did not enjoy the barely managed terror of the descent into the city. I did not slow until I reached the river and even that I crossed while maintaining as much of my momentum as possible.

Many of the bridges had fallen, either in the emergency or its aftermath, but between Union Quay and Morrison's Island, there was a pontoon bridge that would knock at least half an hour off crossing the city. If I had been walking, I probably wouldn't have risked it—the Laoi is brackish even this far from the sea and squid sightings were still reasonably common.

Empowered with a feeling of invincibility from my high-speed descent into the city, I would race across the bridge and up the wooden ramp on the other side, the wooden slats beneath shaking my brain in its pan and the stink of the undredged river condensing in my nostrils.

The other reason for my haste was so I could spend more time with Grace, the chef at Gamble's restaurant.

The front of Gamble's faced the Mall, but deliveries were made to the rear, on Phoenix Street, across a void in the city like a pulled tooth.

The day I fell in love with her I signaled my arrival by dropping my panniers onto the stainless steel kitchen table and in she walked, slender and considered in her chef's whites, her hair tied in a bun behind her head. She made straight for a little aluminum percolator and produced two perfect coffees. God knew where she got the beans from, but it alone would have made my three-hour round trip worth it, so I sat and sipped and waited for her to finish her inspections.

First she smelled each bunch of leaves, tucking a stray, black coil of hair behind her ear. The faintest whiff of rot or smear of leaf slime and she might have dismissed the whole batch.

I raised my cup and smirked. "I cut them myself, this morning."

"That's what you always say," she said, but without malice. She walked to a shelf and returned with some bottles. I knew the drill. Oil, probably rapeseed, a vinegar, cider this time, sea salt shaved so fine you could glaze windows with it. A minute's blurred whisking and she speckled some rocket leaves in the emulsion. She rolled them deftly with her fingers and popped the neat bundle into her mouth.

"It used to be considered an aphrodisiac, you know, rocket," I said, glancing away as she chewed. "Monks were banned from growing it in monastery gardens."

"Well, nobody wants horny monks, I suppose," she said, licking her lips.

Moll referred to one of her tunnels as "the lab." Creedon was right, she had been a bigwig in the University medicine department, but in her lab, Moll applied that science to propagation. She wasn't secretive about her work or the space, but she made it clear enough that she didn't like being disturbed when she was in there.

However, as I passed one evening in early March, I was beckoned in by a clearly excited Moll.

"I've had a bit of a breakthrough," she said. "Come and have a look."

Down one side of the tunnel, beds with soils of varying colors and richness were marked out in square-foot blocks using sticks and twine. At the center of each square, one plant grew, protected and mulched by a thick coil of straw drawn from a large stack kept between the lab and the next tunnel.

On the other side of the narrow path, benches held a dozen or more large green crates that had been repurposed as growing trugs. From the stenciled codes on their sides, they had clearly once held weapons or ammunition of some type. But now they were filled with pale and puckered earth, from which an ugly, scrawny plant poked through at fairly even intervals.

"A couple of years ago, a fellow called Furio, one of the Sicilians, brought me something, a curiosity really, that he wanted me to see if I could grow."

My first thought was it was weed or tobacco. The Bishops would not be pleased if the Monks on Garnish Island lost their monopoly.

Reading my expression, she said: "It's a kind of fodder crop. Very old, very rare, but just a herb really."

The plant was not much to look at, a lanky yellow weed such as you would see poking from any of a hundred ditches within a mile of the farm.

"And?"

"And I've bloody done it. Twasn't easy, it's a very finicky plant, loves its own soil and nothing else and harder than a huckleberry to take viable cuttings from."

She pointed to the crates.

"You know how embassies used to say 'you are now on American soil,' or British soil, or whatever, but it was just a metaphor? This soil is straight from Cyrene, in what was once Libya," she said. "Libya's gone 30 years and Cyrene a lot longer than that. Up to now, in these crates is the only place we know of that this stuff grew. In that dirt."

Among the tools I had seen in Maura's milking shed was a slean—a spade for cutting turf, with a long metal channel, L-shaped in cross-section. It was used to slice a long cake of turf from the cutting face of a bog, which the turf-cutter would then sling onto a pile to dry.

The Sicilians looked like they had done something similar, but horizontally, cutting long, deep strips of topsoil, plants and all, and depositing them in the munitions cases.

"What's it called," I asked.

"The Romans called it silphium, and Nero himself was supposed to have eaten the last of it."

Towards the end of my second full summer with Moll, I had established a mostly enjoyable routine. I would deliver in the city three or four times a week and snatch an hour with Grace when I could. Then I would come home and help Moll prepare for our new venture into livestock. Lambs first, but after that, who knew?

Before the animals arrived in spring, there were fences to mend, feed to arrange, and growing tunnels to clear, so that we could plant out more silphium cuttings.

Once in a while, under the pretense of delivering old chip fat for Moll's biodiesel reactor, Grace would drive out and stay the night at the farm. If Moll was surprised or scandalized, she didn't let on.

One such evening, I was showing Grace the beds. We weeded while we chatted, just for something to busy the hands, before hearing Moll's clomping step across the ridged concrete of the farmyard. Behind her walked a couple, difficult to age, but reasonably well dressed, and a young girl of about 15. Led by the girl, on a piece of fraying orange washing line, followed a scrawny white lamb.

Moll nodded a salute to myself and Grace, but the rest of the group paid us no heed as they padded somberly past.

"Who were they?" asked Grace.

I shrugged. I knew Moll was occasionally consulted by other farmers and market gardeners to help with planting plans, and at least one old fella had asked her advice on his daughter's marriage plans. Visitors were rare, but not unheard of.

"I'd lay you pounds to pence that girl was expecting," said Grace.

"Oh yeah?"

"Yeah."

By now, Grace had stopped pulling weeds and sat on the wooden wall of the bed, her gaze drilling into Moll's front door.

"They didn't look very happy about it," she said.

I shrugged again. "She's pretty young."

"Still. The country needs people," Grace said as she worried at a splinter in the board beneath her hand.

I didn't know what to say to that. Looking back on it now, I suppose I knew what was going on, but while that girl, nor any of the subsequent ones, did not leave in what I would call a happy frame of mind, each left looking a little less ground down by unintended or unwanted consequences.

"Do you ever want children?" she said, after a while.

I laughed, and I suppose she took that as my answer.

Before long, Moll's consulting party left her rooms and showed themselves to the gate, mother, father, and daughter—their three heads still down, their tread still soft, and minus one lamb.

By the end of that October, we had two full tunnels given over to cuttings of the herb. They would be ready for our stock lambs, due up from Dingle in February for finishing.

But for now, we had that first girl's lamb. Moll had me feed it barley meal and alfalfa hay, mixed with some of the silphium she had grown in her "lab." The plant didn't smell unduly when you cut it out of the soil, but when you crushed it to mix with the lamb's food, by God it stank. Like a wet woolen sock you had used to wipe up old fish.

After about a month, Moll determined that the lamb had enough meat on it to be worth the pot. Although her experiment was as yet unproven, rearing any meat at all was prodigal enough in those days to be cause for a party.

At my suggestion, Grace would cook. Moll invited Furio, the Cyrenian who had given her the plants, and Mrs. Weber, the chaperone from the yellow house where we had met, plus Creedon was to be there, along with a host of other friends and associates.

The day of the party, work was long and dull, carrying out my normal duties as well as dressing the barn with a makeshift table, some old benches, and whatever wildflowers and oil lamps I could muster. But I was looking forward to the feast, and to seeing some friends.

Everyone wore their finest rig-outs and the tables heaved with food. Goat cheeses from north Cork, farmed trout from over the Crosshaven hills, oatcakes with honeycomb from the apiary on top of the old school of commerce in the city. Everyone Moll had ever fed, it seemed, was here, and everyone had brought something, either to eat or to drink.

This time, Moll needed no flourish to get proceedings started. Everyone knew why they were there. The lamb's legs and shoulders would be roasted, chops and cutlets grilled, neck stewed, the pluck minced and made into a pudding with oats and herbs, then boiled, like a haggis or a white pudding.

But the first test of our labors was to be a loin fillet, and to make the test fair, Moll had paid for the same cut from a city butcher.

Grace indicated two plates. Each of the loins was perfectly cooked, seared to the color of teak. Grace had cut each into nine or ten mouthfuls, showing the contrast between the colored bark and the intimately pink flesh inside.

"This is the normal lamb, come up from Dingle a week or so ago, it ate nothing but Kerry scrub. This is Moll's lamb, fed with her wonder herb."

Moll glared at her as if she were sharing industrial secrets, but we were among friends and I thought no more of it.

By sight alone, I couldn't tell which was which, but taste did the work of the other senses here. I elbowed my way to the table, forked a piece of the Dingle lamb and put it in my mouth.

It was delicious, and if that was where the treats ended that evening, I think I would have been happy.

Then I tried a piece of Moll's lamb.

I would call it indescribable, but everything is describable. I just lacked the vocabulary then.

If you asked me now, what I would say is that there is always a gap between a review, or a critique, or even just an honestly expressed groan of delight at eating something, and that food's honest, naked taste.

Fresh cheese on warm bread, blood sausage and onions, a trout still a-twitch with life as it hits a pan of hot butter. The taste of all these things is wonderful, but describable.

With Moll's lamb, that gap between expectation and actuality was so big as to render me temporarily dumb. The flesh was meltingly sweet, but not one-dimensional sweetness like a finger dipped in sugar. This was the honey of a just overripe mango, it was a flavor distilled from fragrance. As the tongue probed beyond that, there were earthy notes, an almost decayed saltiness, like fish sauce or miso.

But back then, in Minane, my experience of those tastes and my ability to put all that into words was still a continent and a decade away.

Sitting in the mundane, functional surroundings of Moll's barn, all I could manage was: "I don't think I have ever eaten anything quite as wonderful as that."

I was not alone. Wordlessly, Moll bade Grace and Furio try it.

Furio's face was illuminated as if by a spiritual fluorescence, but he said nothing. I attributed his silence either to him being overwhelmed with the survival of some small part of his birthland or the knowledge of how much money he would get for meat of this quality.

Grace pronged one of the remaining pieces of meat and I expected the chef, the trained palate, the perfectionist, to critically and dispassionately fill the gaps I could not. Instead, she resorted to simple blasphemy: "Jesus. I mean, Jesus."

After the taste test, the evening followed the normal trajectory. People ate and drank, and were merry and rambunctious and talked of happier times, either behind us and how we missed them or ahead of us and how we may get there.

At such evenings in the city, Maura rarely showed any interest in this chat and this was no different. She sat and grimaced in boredom at the politics, the endless plans, and picked at the toughened skin of the mallet finger on her left hand, but never volunteered a word.

Grace, feeling secure in alcohol on what she should have known was treacherous ground, would not let such passivity lie, however.

"Do you not want to join us in rebuilding our country, Maura?" she asked, her tone too smug, too expectant.

Moll looked at her coolly, a teacher sizing up a student, unsure whether or not she was worth the time it would take to educate.

"I suppose I don't," she said eventually.

Moll blinked, eyeing the assembled as if a buzzard choosing gobbets. She continued: "Although I suppose it depends on what you mean by 'rebuild' and who you mean when you say 'our.' I just want to look after my farm in peace. I have friends and I have food and that is a vast improvement on the times I had neither."

This was Moll at her most magnanimous. These days, I could have read the strain in the faces around me and the mix, in Maura's face, of resignation and a feral delight that somebody was pressing the issue, forcing the lethal gunslinger out of retirement. But I didn't have such diplomatic senses then. Nor did Grace. She had been offered a final "nobody has to get hurt" way out, but she lacked the sense to take it.

She tried earnestness, almost always a mistake with Moll: "Do you not understand, Maura? We need people, Maura. We need them to rebuild."

Moll looked straight at me and all I could think of was a girl leaving without her lamb.

"That may be true," she said, holding my gaze, "but you can't just be forcing people to make more people, can you, Grace?"

Grace persisted: "Well, I just wonder what you're growing all this wonderful food for, if not to feed those of us at least trying to repopulate our wonderful country."

She interrupted Grace at volume, and the happy drone of the party withered into silence.

"Wonderful country? What would you know about that, without a child or a parent buried? I'd rather have more food and fewer people than the other way around. So would anyone with any sense. In any case, you seem to be doing your best to repopulate this wonderful country all on your own. Is the food better at this party, chef, or do you miss your German noodles?"

At this point, a few people broke into nervous laughter, catching Moll by surprise. She holstered her tongue.

I could say nothing. If this was true, how did I not know? Why had Grace not told me? Or Moll, for that matter? And if it were not, how could Moll try to hurt me like that?

Mrs. Weber, ever the host, walked over, smiling sweetly, and touched Maura on the arm: "That's all right, Moll."

With considerably more menace, she turned to Grace: "I'd like to talk to you outside for a moment."

I followed them both out into the courtyard, incensed, although unsure where to direct it.

"So you're another one happy for this nation to wither and die, are you," Grace said, viciously indignant at the entitlement of the elderly, who had known a country measured in millions rather than thousands.

Mrs. Weber held up an imperious hand and waited for her to stop spluttering.

"Moll lost her sister, her daughters and her mother in '36 and her husband a year or two later. Maybe lay off the 'glorious repopulation' stuff, OK, chef? Or fuck off back to town."

Her gracious smile returned without effort and she left me, standing in the moonlight, gaping at Grace.

"Tell me she's lying," I said.

"I can't."

"You've been going to the famine parties?"

"I have."

"In God's name, why?"

"Because I want children, I want my mother to have grandchildren, I want a future, I want to be safe. You can't give me all that, can you? I'm not sure you would even if you could."

I said nothing.

Grace kissed me once, on the cheek, but my hands stayed firmly at my sides.

"I'll see you," she said.

By April, the word was out. "Minane lamb" was being ordered from as far away as Kilkenny and orders were such that I had graduated from prehistoric bicycle to prehistoric van to make my deliveries in town. Rather than call at Gambles first to see Grace, I made that stop the last of my day, in the hope that she would be on a prelunch break. In any case, the vehicle made such noise pulling into the yard behind the restaurant that she had ample notice of my arrival and I had not bumped into her in months.

As the orders had increased over the late winter and early spring, so too did the frequency of families with young girls, or sometimes lone women, calling on Moll for advice. The price of this advice wasn't always a lamb, of course—that's just how the story went afterwards. It was often a hen, or a pheasant, or a fat salmon that somebody brave or foolhardy had pulled from the River Ilen. Sometimes, the advice and the treatment were free.

Between the increased activity on both fronts, I suppose it was inevitable that somebody would show up asking questions.

On my return from the city one morning, two middle-aged men stood casually above the crossroads on the road up to the farm. The elder and better dressed of the pair raised a heavy walking stick, as if to hail a passing traveler.

"Well, you're not Maura anyway," he said cheerfully when I stopped. The accent wasn't local, but I couldn't quite place it. "We're only after some lamb."

He walked over to the van, the lack of a limp marking the stick as a weapon rather than a crutch. He was meticulously clean-shaven, a neck scrubbed pink with cheap-smelling soap and where his hand rested on the open window, I could see his fingernails were cut meticulously square. His associate was scruffier and altogether more nervous looking, and the pair of them screamed "policeman."

What could I do? I was already on the road and the gate was chained in front of me. A narrow boreen led off to the right, but the van would have struggled up the hill even without the prodigious undergrowth.

"Follow me up so," I said, hoping that if they were policemen, they were looking for a bribe—some free chops or, at worst, a cut of the proceeds.

They were only seconds behind me as I reached the gate. I hopped down from the van to unchain it, and they were next to me before I could think.

"I'm afraid if it's the Minane lamb you're after, we're sold out."

Leaning on his stick and with his bottom lip stuck out in an expression of crestfallen insincerity, the elder man said: "Oh that's a shame, but I hear Moll is a woman who can help a girl in need of a miracle."

"I don't know about all that," I said as confidently as I could, struggling with the lock.

"Well, it's not the lamb I'm after, really," he continued. "I suppose what I'm really after are the people who are bringing ye the lambs."

"Oh, like our suppliers, you mean?"

I don't recall if my slowness in unlocking the gate was pretense or whether the fellow had me so rattled I couldn't unhook it, but either my glib answer or my delay in admitting him prompted him to act.

Without warning, he brought the heavy length of ash down on my forearm. I won't pretend I heard the snap over my scream, but from the sensation of grating wrongness in moving it afterwards, I knew he had broken it.

He was almost apologetic in his tone: "Did ye really think no one would tell a neighbor, that no one would confess to a priest? That Dr. Verane could play god out here on her farm when she knows we need people more than we need food?"

His colleague ripped the keys from my grasp, undid the lock, and chipped in: "So let's try again without the smart mouth, shall we? Where's Maura Verane?"

The first one prodded me once in the damaged arm with his cudgel and waved me up the path to the farmyard. Then he handed the stick to his colleague and withdrew a pistol from inside his jacket, marking him out as an ideologically pure "detective" rather than just a nosey and bribable guard.

We walked into the middle of the yard, his gun occasionally poking me from behind.

"Come on out, Moll," he called. "Don't make me put a pill in your helper here."

But no response came.

Again he jabbed me with the barrel. "Where might she be?"

Enough time has passed that I feel no shame now, but at the time I was so terrified that he was going to kill me I would probably have given them anything. He didn't need me. One can only assume they would have tried Moll and executed her eventually, but there was nothing to stop him from terminating my existence on the spot and dumping me in a septic tank somewhere.

"She might be in her lab," I offered.

"Ah, the source of the 'cure.' Show me."

He directed his colleague to inspect the far end of the yard as we walked past the raised beds, the cold frames, and most of the silphium-bearing tunnels until we reached Moll's lab.

The large plastic flap at the front was tied up, usually a sign that she was working, but as the detective ushered me in first, I could see she wasn't present. Her colored mohair coat hung on the back of her chair, but of Moll there was no sign.

"No Moll, huh? Isn't this awful altogether," he said, grinding the gun into my kidney.

"Come on Moll, you're almost famous," he called out. "We've come all the way down the country to see you."

"Jeez, she's very quiet," he said softly to me. Then he paused to listen for his mate, but there was not a sound from across the yard.

"Ronan," he called. No answer came.

"Ronan, where in the fuck are you?" he shouted.

With his free hand, he shoved me viciously between the shoulder blades and I stumbled over the threshold of the tunnel and into the farmyard beyond, twisting a foot in a drainage channel and ending up flat on my back. I screamed at the flash of pain from my arm as I watched him emerge.

He stepped out and over the piece of wood that had tripped me up. In that moment, with all of his attention on where he was placing his feet, he did not see Moll rise like some nightmarish, bloody monster from the mound of hay between the tunnels. She took two steps towards him in her bare feet and the first hint the Dublin policeman had of her presence was when the point of the rusty sickle bit into the left side of his neck.

Something vital had been severed and he fell without another word. But Moll, just to be sure, raised the weapon in her other hand, the bloody half-filled bottle of oil that she had used to dispatch "Ronan," and beat him repeatedly about the head until he was still.

I don't know if Moll had been planning this specific escape, or always stood ready to flee, but within minutes she had washed in a rain barrel by her door, changed clothes, and "borrowed" the battered old truck from Buckley's.

On our own van and truck, she had opened up the fuel caps and run rags soaked in lamp fuel into the tanks. She had spread straw and hay in all the tunnels and after we had dragged the bodies into her own quarters, gave them and it a good dousing in diesel. She had a pan of oil heating on the gas stove, ready to kick over and get the whole thing going.

She was loading Buckley's truck with jerry cans full of biodiesel, boxes of fresh and dried food, and bottles of water. In the open bed, secured between hessian bags of damp compost, were four or five dozen potted silphium plants.

Attached to each pot was a card of instructions in Maura's simple script.

"Grind up a handful of the leaves and berries, mix them with some apple juice or some brandy, add a bit of honey to take the edge off the stench of it, and swallow.

"Take it daily until the cramps kick in. You'll know when it's done. Tell nobody but those who need to be told."

That was more detailed instruction than she had given me.

"Anyone asks, you fell while having tea with Mrs. Buckley, right? First you knew of trouble was when you saw the flames and I stole her truck. In a few days, go talk to Mrs. Weber about a job. OK?"

Once the van was loaded, there were no hugs, no farewells. Moll kicked over the gas stove, waited until she was sure the main house and every tunnel was well alight, jumped in the truck, and was gone.

Mrs. Buckley walked me down the hill "for sweet tea and to ring the fire brigade."

"Stop the car, I'd prefer to walk in," I said. The small electric Tata pulled to the side of the pitted and gravelly road, I opened the door and I walked into Minane for the first time in 30 years.

It is still quiet—no buildings had been added, but nor had any collapsed, and many were roofed with the new perovskite panels, so I knew they were lived in, cared for.

I passed the church and its small graveyard, where I recognized a scrubby yellow plant growing between the graves. Like a huckleberry, Moll said, it would only grow in undisturbed earth: "They grow free or they don't grow at all."

I don't know if it was a final "up yours" to the authorities, or just poetic irony, but now, even with better, safer alternatives available out of the east, every churchyard and cemetery in the country still harbors Moll's plant.

Past the church, I rounded the corner at Buckley's Bar and wondered what had become of Mary, the first of the two women who saved me.

Above the cross, the outline of Moll's farm was still there, under weeds and ivy. I had thought it may have been razed and grassed over. The uncovered and blackened hoops that used to support the grow tunnels still ran at right angles from the road, stretching from just beyond the low, roofless farmhouses to the crest of the hill, as if someone had tried to stitch the landscape together with long lines of staples.

Below the small field, where we kept the lambs—the miraculous and the other kind—I stopped.

Nobody I've spoken to knows where Maura Verane is buried. In every home from Kilmore to Kinvarra, you will hear a different story about how Moll met her end: She was thrown by a mob from the cliffs in Clare, to be consumed by the mechanical squid that roam the Atlantic yet; the priests burned her as a heretic in the basement furnace of a Galway church; she fled for America in an aerostat; or she wanders the west coast still, planting her "cure" as she goes. I'd like to believe that last one, but it would put her in her early hundreds.

Moll is almost certainly dead. Despite the stories, for most of our time at the farm, we never grew anything much more exotic than coriander. It burned anyway.

But should a pilgrimage be on your mind, that verdant field at Minane Bridge would be a good place to start.

I turned to lean my back against the stone and sod wall, my breath stolen from me, my cheeks wet. Perhaps I wasn't as ready to sift ashes as I thought.

As I lay there on the ditch, watching the clouds scud past the tree line that marked the top of the hills opposite, a lone boy and his dog walked down the boreen towards me, neither creature anywhere near as rare as they were when I lived here, but still unusual enough for me in these surroundings to put a catch in the throat.

I tried to smile at the boy.

"Good morning. Do you live around here?" I said.

"Mornin'. Are you American?"

"No, but I can see why you might think that. My accent has changed a lot. I used to live around here, actually."

"Really?"

"Yes, for a while. Do you know whose farm that was?" I said, gesturing to the ruin behind me.

He stopped to consider the question with a suspicious turn to his head. I ruffled the dog's dishwater pelt while I waited for him to figure out how varnished his response should be.

"I do," he said finally, puffing his chest out: "Mad Moll." There is always a pride, a vicarious notoriety, in living close to a famous or infamous person, even if only in location rather than in time.

I couldn't help but grin. I never knew her as that, however much I had occasionally agreed with the sentiment.

"Who is Mad Moll?" I asked.

"Moll of Cyrene," he said, as if only a fool would not know, "like the song." Then in mock exasperation, and with dancing hands, he intoned " . . . six guards she killed, they're lying still, at the bridge in Minane town, she found the cure, that cute old hoor, that brought the bishops down . . . "

Two bad bastards who got what was coming to them had become six policemen. In another thirty years, it may be a dozen.

"And where is she now?" I asked, wondering if I would get a new theory on her disappearance or a pastiche of one I had already collected.

"I dunno," he said. "Dead, I suppose."

"You're probably right," I said. I extended my hand for help in hauling my carcass off the damp ditch and we began walking down the hill to Minane, to the waiting car and my wife.

"So, tell me, can you teach me this song?"

ABOUT THE AUTHOR

Finbarr O'Reilly is an Irish speculative fiction writer who likes to explore how broken technologies or unearthly events affect intimate locales. Why would you want to write about alien battleships invading New York when you can imagine little green men asking for directions from a short-tempered undertaker in Carrigtwohill, Co Cork?

He has previously been published in *Clarkesworld* and in the anthologies *The Best Science Fiction of the Year,* edited by Neil Clarke, and *The Year's Best Science Fiction,* edited by Gardner Dozois.

Finbarr has worked as a journalist for almost twenty years, most of those as a sub-editor (copy-editor).

Like many Irish writers, Finbarr lives in self-imposed exile. He currently resides with his wife and two children in a small town in Lincolnshire, UK, too far from the sound of gulls and the smell of saltwater.

Sparrow

YILIN WANG

The rooftop is quiet except for the hum of a plane passing overhead, heading to a faraway elsewhere. The sharp stench of ammonia rises from the bucket hanging from your window-cleaning belt. Running your fingers across the safety harness and clips that encircle your chest and back, you triple check all the safeguards to ensure they are all locked in place. You pull yourself over the icy metal railing and lean back. Safety ropes and the padding of your wooden bosun's chair hold your weight. Chongqing sprawls out beneath your dangling feet and the hazy pollution. It's a muted miniature world of glass and steel, encircled by snaking rivers that divide the city center from the satellite cities and the blue mountains beyond.

After three years of drifting down Chongqing's skylines, this will be your last descent.

On the grime-covered window in front of you, Sparrow Li's face appears instead of your own. She scales walls and jumps across rooftops in a single leap, with no need for a single rope. Centuries ago, she stole silver taels from the wealthiest duke to give to beggars, slaves, and peasants, leaving only a folded paper sparrow behind to claim the deed. If you were her, you wouldn't have to worry about buying enough rice to feed yourself.

Sparrow disappears as you wipe the window clean with a squeegee. Your bangs have grown long and unruly again despite your attempts to tame them with rusty scissors. The black eye bags beneath your scrawny angular face are so dark they look like gothic makeup. Carefully, you make your way down, cleaning each window until you reach the outside of your boss' office.

The boss stands with his back to you. With both hands, he grips a machine shaped like a hexagonal ship's wheel. You saw an image of it recently in a trade magazine in his office: a newly-invented window cleaning drone. Unlike he said days ago, he isn't firing you because he found cheaper labor, but because he has decided that a robot is better than you.

You bang your squeegee loudly on the window until he cracks it open.

"Stop that," he says. "You're going to break the glass. Is something wrong?"

"What happened to firing me to save costs? The drone costs at least twice my salary."

He places his drone down on a table. Awkward silence slips in among you like an uninvited uncle who refuses to leave. "I'm sorry. I'm sure you'll find another job. This work is too dangerous anyways, for a young woman like you."

Your profession has been crumbling over the past year; children once followed their parents into the business, but no more. Cleaning windows is too dangerous, too tiresome, too much labor for too little pay. Yet for drifters like you, it's the best option you have.

He's a migrant too, a fellow drifter from your shared hometown of Luo Dai. In his late twenties, only a few years older than you. When he landed his manager job weeks ago, he bragged that he had just graduated with a master's degree from Beijing University, the dream school you wrote an essay about attending in grade four. When your teacher laughed at your paper and your parents told you to find a more realistic goal, you folded the pages into a paper boat and threw it into the Yangtze River.

"Come on, please, would you reconsider? You must understand how hard it is to find a job in Chongqing. Give me another chance."

Seven years ago, a few months before high school graduation, you dropped out, taking a bus and train and another bus to move to Chongqing. All you carried were two bags and three crumbled one hundred renminbi bills. Barely enough for a month's rent in the cheapest shared dorm.

Before you left Luo Dai, you had glanced back from the bus. Mama coughed up blood from an illness no doctor in town could identify. Baba could barely stand and leaned against his cane. If you stayed, you would only end up like them, your days weighed down by bricks of debt, unable to find well-paid work in the countryside.

"You don't have to go," Baba said. "You should stay and finish school, instead of going off to work."

"My cousins went," you replied. "I'll settle down in a metropolis and send money. Eventually, I'll be able to bring you to the city with me. All will be well."

As the bus jostled off, past rice fields drying up from drought and huts crumbling from disrepair, you met Sparrow Lee the first time in a battered volume of folktales. She wandered the rivers and lakes of Middle Kingdom long ago. She had no ties to family or land, no silver or heirlooms. Her lack of anything gave her the freedom to become anybody.

In Chongqing, you met countless others like you, a thousand migrants flocking here each day from towns with names you didn't know. Everyone calls those like you the piaozhu, drifters. Some drifters, those in the tier-one megacities of Beijing and Shanghai, have nicknames with their city names incorporated: the ones in Beijing are bei-piaozhu, the ones in Shanghai are hai-piaozhu.

But here, you are only piaozhu. You find comfort in the enormity of the word, in the anonymity that comes with belonging to a group without a place name.

Simply to drift, unattached to a city, is enough.

In the makeshift dorm room that you still share with four other drifters, your roommates offered you pumpkin seeds to snack on, tales of long train rides with standing-room tickets, photos of younger siblings left behind. The crowded lifestyle is called yiju, ant living, because so many of you gather like ants in a hill. Although small, ants can carry ten times their weight. When the paths of ants are blocked, they always find alternate routes.

The staring contest between you and your boss is interrupted by a young woman who leans into the doorway across the room. She waves her right hand. Her left hand holds her camera, and three heavy lenses poke out of her shoulder bag like ancient brass telescopes. You grip your safety ropes tighter, leaning into the open window.

The photographer has come to take photos for her "Drifters in Chongqing" page on New Waves, where she has three hundred thousand followers. She called your boss a week ago, on the day after you had received your layoff notice, asking him for permission to trail you for photos on the final day. Initially, you cringed at the request. When the photographer shared that she was alone in the city too, without any family, you relented.

"Smile and look cheerful in front of the photographer," your boss says. "You'll look terrible if you're scowling."

You glance at your reflection in the window again and run your hands through your tangled hair. "Try not to make me look too sad."

"Look down and away. Show all your sadness and nostalgia and vulnerability. Don't be shy, reveal all your buried feelings so that my followers can empathize with you."

You move mutely in response to her requests. She peers at you through her viewfinder. She tugs your limbs like a puppet master, directing you until your body seems no longer your own. Click, click, click.

"Are you sure this will help? I'm a window cleaner, not a model. All the posing feels so unnatural."

"Don't worry, I'll write a note with my photo and tag you. Maybe another drifter will see your story and help you out."

"I've got to start working. Take pictures while I work, up in the air."

Before she can reply, you pull your rope once and descend to the next window. You dip your largest squeegee into soap water. Sweep it across the window, a painter priming the first layer of your canvas. Switching your squeegee for a smaller one, you swirl it atop the foaming surface. As you wipe away bubbling soap, you paint a scene of a paper boat drifting down the banks of the Yangtze River, disappearing among riverboats and steamers, sinking down until it mingled with purple freshwater jellyfish. You touch the foam with your fingertips before obliterating it with another swipe of your squeegee, leaving the glass blank, sparkling clean. The window art you paint is fragile like Sparrow's paper sparrows.

When you peer down, thousands of apartments tower over the city streets, identical boxes differentiated by colorful laundry hanging from lines and potted plants. Windows open and doors sway, offering brief glimpses into other lives. Bunk beds and tabletop stoves crowd claustrophobic rooms. Ancient radios stand on desks, their antennas extended in search of signals.

Beneath you, on the ground, ant people scurry past one another without stopping. They intersect and diverge with surprising speed. You long to drop your rope all the way down and stop in front of each, ask where they're from and where they're going. No one has time to glance up at you, except for the photographer standing at the foot of the skyscraper, her telephoto lens raised in your direction.

When you first arrived in the city, you spent days job hunting without a single offer letter. All you needed was one guanxi, one connection, so you knocked on doors: the aunty who had also moved here from Luo Dai, the older alumnus-brother who attended your high school, the sworn sister of your cousin who drifted to Chongqing a year before you did. None of those doors led anywhere.

"If you find it too difficult in Chongqing, you can come home," Mama said in a phone call. "I know how hard it is to build a life over there. Perhaps we're just meant to lead difficult lives." She always read your mood even when you didn't tell her.

"I can't give up," you replied. "Not after coming all this way."

Restaurant owners turned you down because you weren't slim enough to be a hostess. Construction sites answered they only wanted muscular men able to lift fifty kilograms up a flight of stairs. Retail stores demanded you produce a high school diploma. You landed a temporary job as a dishwasher in a cafe, only to be laid off a month later without your final wages.

Eventually, after more weeks of temporary work, a guanxi called you with news. He knew a company that wanted to hire a permanent window cleaner. They struggled to find someone because they needed an employee who didn't fear heights and was willing to risk their life for a paycheck.

You said you'd love it.

On your trial day, you bent over the edge of this skyscraper's rooftop, stomach churning, knees trembling. Staring at the steep drop and the ant people below, your head spun with vertigo. Even Sparrow had to work to make a living in rougher days; besides robbing dukes of silver, Sparrow worked as a mercenary, wielding a sword in exchange for copper coins and a bed in an inn. With her by your side, you grasped the ropes with the tightness of a rock climber and began your first descent.

The company hired you at the end of that day. To say thank you to your guanxi, you spent half of your first paycheck on the best baijou you could afford. Sweet savory rice wine, the kind recipients kept on a living room mantle for years, passed from one generation to the next.

Near the exit of the skyscraper, your hands cling to your harness and tool belt before handing them over to your boss. Now you'll have to trade drifting down a skyscraper for another type of drifting, the same old days of job searching in Chongqing.

The boss puts a hand on your shoulder. "I'm very sorry. You should consider another line of work, an industry where automation isn't so common. Good luck."

"If the company can do this to me, they can do it to you."

He turns away and walks for the elevator up to his office.

You head for the exit, the photographer dogging your footsteps. "Please let me take a few last photos of you."

"Robots can take photos too. Drones can fly beyond your reach to take aerial images."

"They can't make art."

"Japan invented a robot that wrote a novel," you reply. "It won second place in a novel writing competition."

Her hands shake, and she nearly drops her camera. "That's not the same. Robots might be able to win chess competitions, but they can't fully capture the depths of human emotions."

She shows you the photos taken today. You recognize the way you grin and frown, your limp figure dangling from ropes, a tiny ant lost among high-rises. In the folktales, Sparrow simply vanished in her final days, and no one knows her fate. But you can find a glimpse of Sparrow in those photos. "Send me a link to the photos when you post them up."

When you glance up at the windows of the skyscraper, you see the drone, a disk with six legs. It clings to your boss' window like a spider, with no rope or harness in place. The photographer beside you stares at it too and raises her camera to snap photos. The drone slides across the building's side with fearless efficiency, spraying water and soap, spinning quickly as it wipes the glass. As she snaps photos, you sneak away, and head for the underground train back to your overcrowded dorm.

Tonight, you'll tiptoe out of your dorm to escape your roommates' consolation and dial the number of the same guanxi who helped you land this job. After you ask whether she has eaten dinner, you'll pose the question, "Do you know anyone else who needs a window cleaner?" She'll sigh and ask you to try elsewhere. The harness and tools you once relied on have been stripped from you, leaving you without any safety rope to hold onto. The only wings you have left are the tattered pages of Sparrow's legends, her flight path fracturing with uncertainty, obscured by clouds.

ABOUT THE AUTHOR

Yilin Wang is a Chinese Canadian writer and editor who has lived in China, the U.S., Scotland, and Canada. Her fiction has appeared or is forthcoming in *Clarkesworld, Ricepaper Magazine,* and *What If? Magazine,* while her poetry has appeared in *The Best of Abyss & Apex Vol.2, Grain, Contemporary Verse 2, Cerebration,* and other journals. Her work has placed second for the Spark Literary Prize, as well as been longlisted for The Malahat Review's Far Horizon Award for Short Fiction and TNQ's Peter Hinchcliffe Short Fiction Award. Yilin also serves as an assistant editor for *Room Magazine* and works as the Volunteer Coordinator for Growing Room: A Feminist Literary Festival. She is currently writing an epic fantasy novel inspired by Chinese martial arts fiction and heroic legends, as well as penning a collection of poetry on travel and displacement. When she is not writing, you can find her drinking matcha, watching animated films, and planning her next trip overseas.

When We Were Starless

SIMONE HELLER

When we set out to weave a new world from the old, broken one, we knew we pledged the lives of our clutches and our clutches' clutches to wandering the wastes. Season after season, our windreaders find us a path through the poison currents, and our herds scuttle over molten glass seas and pockmarked plains into the haunted places where the harvest is plentiful. We move swiftly, outpacing vapors and packs of wild dogs alike, leaving only the prints of our tails in acrid sands.

This wasn't entirely true; we left other things, too, dear and precious. But this was how it was told by the elders when the veiled moon was high and we were cuddled up with our cozy-stones.

On the moonless nights, though, they spoke of ghosts: beckoning wraithlights and treacherous silent ones, and all the other types we had classified; and the multitudes that still waited for our soothing hands out among the ruins. They spoke of ghosts like they were the ones to handle them, when it was always me.

So when Warden Renke strode up to my resting place on the outskirts of the half-shaped camp, the stark white paint of her dread-screen slapped on in haste, I knew what she needed.

"Someone found another ghost, yes?" My longing glance went to the grub'n'root stew some kind soul had left next to the pack serving as my pillow, still lukewarm from a hot stone placed at the bottom of the bowl. I reached for the harness with my tools instead.

"It's in the dome structure to the East. Asper ventured there in search of the light metals his weaver prefers. He meant no harm; he knows we need every spare part he can churn out. Said he saw strange lights."

"Alright." It could be nothing, or just another minor ghost which I would have laid to rest before the deep-night chill encroached. I stood and fingered my engraved pliers, waiting for Renke to disappear like they all did when it came to my work. But the Warden fixed me, her pupils mere slits.

"Eat your fill first, Blessed. We need you to stay strong. Truss won't be able to step in for you."

And he hadn't stepped in for years now, since the day he became a respected member of the tribe, but I didn't say that.

"How is he?" I asked instead.

Renke looked back to where the first weaverspun tentpoles came together, as if she could see the pallet there, the thin mat of woven vines stained with blood. "He's barely conscious. You should visit him as soon as you've cleansed yourself."

It could well be my last chance. One shift in the weather, and we'd be running again, leaving our excess baggage behind. Truss never passed up an opportunity to teach a lesson, so it would probably be me he'd ask for the Song of Passing, and I was afraid it would be more than I could take. People's hearts, as hardened and as barred as they were, were a different matter from the hearts of ghosts. I took one big mouthful of stew and swallowed. "I'll take care of this ghost, Warden. This spot will serve as a fine resting place and see us recovered to full strength."

Renke cast a doubtful glance down at her freshly spun leg brace, for she, too, hadn't walked away unscathed. "Report to me when it's done. I'll put harvesting on hold, so hurry. No way to know how long the winds will grant us."

The run-in with the rustbreed had not been my fault. I was a good enough scout—I scoured inaccessible ruins for scarce materials, and I never ran the tribe into the lairs of the befouled crablion or let anyone's mind become ghost-shifted. But when the heat-baked ground of a salt flat we were crossing was suddenly riddled with burrower holes, a full legion of the writhing, rearing centipedal creatures already upon us, all I could do was to change the gentle hum of the Lope Concord to the jarring trill of the Rush and find us a path out of this trap. The air had been filled with the dry stick sounds of the rustbreed's milling legs and the sharp smell that went for communication among them. But for all their legs, we were the better runners, and we made it. Barely. The hindquarters of our sole gearbeast were a fused mass of metal and dried fluids from a rustbreed feeder, and I didn't want to think about Truss' side, which had been similarly exposed. Others, like Renke, had been burned badly, too, but he had been the only one to suffer a bite and get the corrosive substance under his scales.

The ruined place I had led us into was vast and violent, some of its canyons carved by storms and some designed by its unholy builders long ago. We had been following these shadowed paths for hours, paths I would have preferred to scout before bringing in the tribe. As it was, I had to lay ghosts to rest on the run, which was a contradiction in and of itself.

I skirted the camp, listening to the whirring sounds of dozens of weavers busily spinning pots and ropes and all the things we would need to shelter and recover. Bits of Asper's cleansing chant drifted over the jagged scenery. He would be fine. Surely he had run at first sight, not even checking if it was a real ghost, or just a reflection on an unexpectedly untarnished surface. It took more than that to risk ghost-shifting. But the tribe was skittish. He would sing half of the night.

Out of the rubble and partially collapsed buildings around the camp, two ruined structures protruded into the upper airs like teeth, broken and half-melted. Loose material flung up by the poison winds had merged with the original walls like flowstone.

No such thing marred the surface of the dome. Its sides were certainly blackened like everything else, and even blacker holes yawned where some of its hexagonal segments were missing, but the telltale pockmarks to determine downwind shelter were nowhere to be seen. It loomed over the rubble as if to claim some things were unbreakable, no matter what. We would prove it wrong, if I had my way and we stayed. Because that was what we did; we cleansed the ruins by harvesting them, by feeding their very substance to our weavers and rendering it pure and useful to be sold to the settler townships up in the mountains.

Only this time we would need every scrap for ourselves to survive.

The entrance to the dome structure was a narrow, curved tube. When I reached a barrier of two thin, clear panes of glass, they swished apart almost soundlessly, releasing a draft of cool air from within. Asper must have been desperate if he had gone beyond that. I took a moment to camouflage and darted through, curling my tail in case of nasty surprises; this would have been a stupid way to lose it. At some point in the past, granules of debris had blown in, but the layer was thin and petered out after a few paces. When the portal closed smoothly behind me, one side grated a little bit on a piece of gravel that must have been displaced by my feet.

My gaze was drawn upwards. The air of the dome was still, the evening light eerily peaceful as it filtered through the once transparent segments. Gone was the cleansing singsong, gone were the high winds keening in cavity-riddled structures. It wasn't that there was no indication of violence in this place: the tail end of a colossal metal tube still hanging from steel cords fastened around its tapered nose had fallen and destroyed all manners of tables and glass cases on the floor. But it was as if it had happened centuries ago, and peace had been found in its arrangement.

Anyone with a healthy fear of ghosts would have gone looking for the one whose invisible hand had moved the glass panes. I knew better. I was not after an inferior ghost tied to this entrance—my prey would be haunting the vast space, where the light was murky and the shadows were glistening. I went straight in to look for the veins that spoke of ghost activity, for the hiding places of ghost organs, stored away in boxes for protection.

Uncomfortably chilly layers of air enshrouded glittering heaps of shards. Once, I might have felt out of place, an unwelcome disturbance. But I had left my fear of ghosts behind like an old skin a long time ago, and what I had found instead was the unforeseen, and sometimes pure beauty.

The tribe never knew. To them, beauty meant nothing. I could have shown them the brightest colors and patterns on my skin, and all they ever wanted were the dulled hues of sand and ashes, all the better to pick clean ruins like this one.

In the end I found absolutely no sign of a ghost inhabiting this space. I resigned myself to take care of the entrance and let go of my camouflage.

When I turned around there was something where there had been no one. Like a person, a solitary figure leaned on one of the undamaged glass cases. The light pooled strangely around it, and when I flicked my tongue, the smell, the heat, and the heartbeat were all my own and told me no other living being was in here with me.

"Hello, little explorer," it said with a clear, slightly hollow voice.

The ways ghosts reacted to people were mostly limited to precise, fatal attacks, if they were of the aggressive kind, or simple things like manipulating doors or following every move with a single red eye in the shell they animated, observant even in afterlife.

This one drifted over to me, mimicking a walk on two legs as best it could, lacking a tail. Its whole body was obscured by a bulky, silvery layer of clothing, its head round like a bowl. It seemed insubstantial, a ghost of subtle dangers. My breath quickened, but I stood my ground. When there was but a pace between us, I lifted my hand to rap my knuckles against the semi-translucent head-bowl with just a hint of bright eyes behind. The ghost quivered slightly as my fingers passed right through it, and on my skin I felt an almost imperceptible sensation of heat.

"Now, now, you're a cheeky one, aren't you?" It turned with me as I began to walk around it, cautiously, looking for the veins tethering its body to its heart. "I understand you're curious, and I encourage you heartily to experiment. But your experience will be better if you refrain from touching me."

The way it reacted to me, seemed to talk directly to me, was disconcerting. I felt a lump grow in my throat. Even now there were no veins. They could still be under the floor, but I somehow doubted it. I had seen a few Untethered before, even sought them out. They didn't need to animate objects, but moved through thin air with a fluid grace. I knew they could be laid to rest with a bit of work; I just chose not to whenever possible. The world always felt lessened by their passing.

"I don't see a tag on you, little explorer." The ghost's voice came from slightly above. So maybe it had stored its lungs somewhere. Finding them would at least be a start. "Would you mind telling me your name to avoid confusion?"

I looked up at the strange specter in surprise. No amount of singing would redeem me in the eyes of my tribe if I volunteered my name to a ghost. Granted, I did talk to ghosts. It was a one-sided conversation, a game of pretending at its best. This ghost wouldn't even register my name, a name nobody had bothered to use since I became Blessed. What harm could it do, to whisper and hear it swallowed up by the still air of the dome?

I flicked my tongue. "Mink. My name is Mink."

The round head bobbed enthusiastically. "Welcome, Mink! Now, would you like to see the stars?"

A flutter of anxiety rose in my stomach. This was more than a mere reaction; this was interaction. For a short moment, I felt this was not a ghost, but something else altogether, something alive and very old and dangerous. I fought my unease with a snort. "Stars? You're trying to trick me with fancy tales the elders tell to hatchlings, yes?"

"That's what most come for, but we can certainly look at something else. The rocket, maybe? Or one of the landers?" It drifted off a little bit, hands clasped behind its back. With a swooshing noise, the soft glow of wraithlights grew throughout the dome, in at least five different places. There were sounds as well, sounds I recognized: ghosts, many upon many of them, animating contraptions, whining in high voices. A legion of ghosts, seemingly springing into action in unison.

I shielded my eyes and staggered back, caught myself on one of the tables, shaken. Such a conglomerate of ghosts would take days to be laid to rest. Our wounded might not have days; they depended on the herds' output before the windreader called us off.

The untethered ghost had moved to hover next to me. "You seem upset, little explorer Mink. Is there something wrong? Something I can do for you?"

I held my face still buried in my hands and looked at the ghost through my fingers. Was it trying to help me? All I had ever been taught told me to run now, but I had never been the student Truss or the other elders had envisioned. "That's impossible . . . "

"Let's try some music to lift your spirits." The ghost drifted back and forth expectantly. When nothing happened and I began to wonder if I should have said or done something, it heaved a great sigh. "Uh . . . I'm very sorry, little explorer Mink . . . some things seem to be amiss here. I thought I had just the right music for you. But now I can't play any at all, and I just don't seem to be able to fix this defect. Ah. I shouldn't be all sad when I need to cheer you up, right? Don't you worry. I'll find a work-around."

"You miss your music?" I had always suspected some ghosts liked music, and tried to use this to my advantage. But this ghost had offered me consolation; it seemed genuinely upset it couldn't act on it. I didn't seek an advantage when I suggested: "I could sing for you."

Truss would have called me ghost-shifted or straight out mad at this point. I had nothing yet, not even a classification, just a growing sense of unease and a lot of work cut out for me. But there were many ways to a ghost's heart, and a nonaggressive, calming approach might work just as well as exhausting oneself by tearing out every wall panel for clues. Or maybe I was just trying to rationalize my own desperate need for a song.

It took some time to find my voice, because, yes, I had sung to ghosts before, but never for a whole legion of them. Soon enough I found the center of the dome was an excellent place to stand and sing.

I did not sing a ghost song, but one of ours. The melody of the Paean of Manifest Horizons rose strongly in the empty air, and it was more uplifting than the somber tones of the Song of Passing I usually sang in the forsaken places of the world, while making them a little bit more forsaken. It wasn't until after the first verse I noticed the second voice accompanying mine in perfect harmony. At first I was puzzled and amused to sing alongside those hidden lungs of the ghost. Then I felt my spirit lifted in a way I had not expected: not to chant alone amongst the rubble of a past age, but to have a voice other than mine echoing, countering, running ahead in joy. When I reshaped the tune into a jubilating variation and the ghost followed suit without pause, though, the dread feeling crept upon me again, made my voice veer off into a warning warble. I faltered, and the ghost sang the ending notes on its own.

Ghosts were the remnants of the long-dead past, and one thing they—or at least all the ones I had encountered—could not do, was evolve, learn, grasp something new. This one had not only learned a song in a few heartbeats, but even how to mold it in the unique way of my tribe. And I finally had my classification and my name, and the absolute certainty that I would not be the one to lay this ghost to rest, or any of its manifestations, for that was what I faced: one vast ghost of many forms, one fabled entity that ruled this whole place. An annihilator of tribes. A Clusterhaunt.

"What an amazing talent," it said, lifting its hand to its chest, where of course no heart resided. "Thank you!"

I tried to swallow against my dried-up throat, but only produced a strangled squawk. When I fled the dome, the ghost called after me: "Little explorer Mink, do you really have to leave already? You haven't seen the stars yet!"

Terrified as I was, I would have crashed into the grating panes of glass. But the ghost moved this extension of itself out of my way, and I stumbled out before it could reconsider.

This was what was going to happen: the camp would be left to the winds, half-shaped pots and tents melting into the ruined landscape. The marrow of our wounded would feed whatever happened to stumble upon this site, our crippled gearbeast would hold its lone wake. I would paint the warning sigil of our tribe on a nearby wall in green permastain, so that no scout in their right mind would ever set foot in the dome again. And we would flee this place, maybe leave a trail of our injured as we ran, and we would never look back, never wonder what we had lost, not only in lives, but also in not taking the rare materials from the dome, in not observing the Clusterhaunt and learning about its ways.

Or at least try to coexist. I had fled on impulse, fueled by the horrors our lore spoke of. It didn't seem so bad now that I had time to think and didn't see a spectral host coming after me from the dome. But how could I suggest this to a tribe who, by that very same lore, left its weakest members behind to die? I would be declared suicidal, a menace, unheard.

For we were survivors, mere survivors; we never managed to be more than that, and some didn't even manage that much. We told ourselves that we made a difference, that we shaped a world, but one look at this ruined vastness told the truth: we didn't change a thing, and all our sacrifices were just to survive another day. It was enough, mostly, as long as we pretended it didn't tear our hearts out.

I was perched on the remains of a toppled roof structure and looked at the bug-catcher lights dotting the camp's perimeter in the dark. They would glow long after we were gone.

When I finally trotted over to the ring of lights, I vocalized a lesser warning sequence. "Scout incoming," I saluted the guard I knew would wait in the shadows beyond. "I need to see Truss. Get someone to apply the dread-screen on him. I'm unclean."

She hissed gruff acknowledgement, and by the time I entered the camp proper every weaver had been moved out of my way, as well as sleeping mats and cooking utensils for good measure. A young herder still gesturing her weaver backwards lifted the eight-legged metal creature up into her arms and staggered away under its weight, even if it was far out of range of whatever evil emanations of mine she might fear. I saw Asper, too, hovering on the fringe of the camp and obviously eager for news, his weaver easy to spot because he was the only one to dread-screen its carapace for extra security. At Truss' resting place, one of the hunters simply smeared the remaining paint in her hands onto her face and throat before I came too close.

On Truss, the swirling white patterns had been applied with more care. He looked bad underneath, skin sagging in stiff folds, eyes sunken. His side was bandaged, the color of the rust-like substance eating away at him already bleeding through.

"Teacher," I said, kneeling next to him.

He lifted one feeble hand, as if to keep me from propping him up. "Talk to the elders, little foster-hatch. Why come to me? They are the ones who decide our way."

They knew only one way, but I didn't say that. "You're one of them, old man. How are you? I was gone so long, and I was afraid you wouldn't . . . "

"Warden told you that, didn't she?" He coughed, and I watched the stains on his bandage deepen. "To keep you on your toes. She knows you're prone to getting distracted."

At that, he winked weakly at me. We had always kept my bolder adventures between the two of us, as we had our differences. I wanted badly to take his hand, to feel if there was any strength left in him, but he had never been fond of touch. Or sympathy.

"I'm not dead yet." His voice was a low rasp. "Won't run for days, but if the winds are willing and you're keeping us safe, I'll eat the stuff that's trying to eat me . . . just you watch."

At that, I felt all color bleed out of my skin and fought hard to keep Truss from noticing. I had been selfish to come here, just so that I could say goodbye. "It might not happen," I offered softly. "It might not happen fast enough. And so many of us are wounded and exhausted. Even I would be hard-pressed to run now."

Part of me wanted to tell him about the Clusterhaunt. But he hadn't scouted for years, and in his day Truss had never been one to indulge in the presence of ghosts. I knew what he would have to say, and I didn't want to hear it.

He said it anyway. "Don't concern yourself with our weak and wounded, little foster-hatch. We're prepared to stay behind, knowing the tribe will survive. The elders are aware of that. They know how to handle it."

"But they don't *have* to handle it," I whispered.

Suddenly I felt Truss' hand on mine, cold and brittle. He started to say something, but in this moment, Renke strode up to us, the windreader and the other two elders in tow.

"What news do you bring, Blessed?" she asked. "Is your work done?"

I looked up at her, then back to Truss. There were days when I found joy in my job, when I felt I brought peace to the ghosts of old and betterment to the brand-new world. Today it felt like laying to rest everything I loved. "My work is never done."

Renke came closer than most dared when I was unclean, to stare down at me. "The herders are awaiting my command. Is it safe now, or do we move?"

There was no invitation to debate, no room for experiments. I only needed to utter the word; the decision was already made, had already been made since the day we set out to wander the wastes.

I fought to keep my unruly colors under control. None of the tribe could actually read them, but Truss had seen most of the spectrum while teaching me, and even with eyes half-closed he might be watching.

Renke's crest rose halfway in impatience. I could feel the eyes of the herders on me, all prepared to set out, their weavers protected in the crooks of their tails. They would never admit that survival was not always enough.

I squeezed Truss' hand one last time and finally got up to look the Warden in the eye. "Send them out," I said. "This place is safe."

• • •

The night sky was a black abyss sucking my gaze upwards, and with it went my bravado and determination. No veiled moon shed its light upon the ruins; the stars, its fabled lesser cousins, were nothing but a story to ease the weight of the dark.

I did not deserve to even think of a soothing story, because I had embarked on the darkest of tales.

Clusterhaunt. Few claimed to have seen one, the even fewer reliable witnesses weren't keen on telling what they had seen. Clusterhaunts were said to be the rarest and mightiest of ghosts, spiteful of the living, and oh-so-strong, the most powerful ghost-shifters, heart-concealers, mind-mimickers.

Tribe-vanishers.

But I had told my lie, and I needed it to turn into truth. So instead of getting back to my lonely resting place, I went to the dome once more. "Residual energies" would keep the herders from entering only for so long; then I would either have found this heart or failed them all.

First I jammed a stone I had brought under the glass panes of the entrance. I didn't want to get trapped inside, and disabling the ghost's extensions piece by piece was one way I figured I could counter its Clusterhaunt abilities. I took my lamp into the pitch-black dome and began to turn over every larger piece of rubble to find a hint of ghostly veins, organs, anything.

All too soon a familiar pale glow came up behind me.

"Little explorer Mink! What a pleasant surprise to have you back!"

I looked up at the bowl-shaped head bobbing above the silvery suit. Why would it choose this appearance when it ruled so many forms? Why not a more threatening one?

It hovered closer. "You were gone so fast last time, I thought you maybe didn't like it. But you've got them both—Curiosity and Spirit. Want to see them? They're right here, brought back to Earth after their duty was done."

Wraithlight flared to life halfway through the dome to illuminate the shapes of two battered gearbeasts. Their odd wheel-legs seemed sturdy enough, but after a closer look, I found them to be perplexingly impractical: their broad backs were plastered with strange contraptions, no room for stowage at all. They wouldn't carry even one of our wounded.

"You'll find the whole story of Curiosity and Spirit on your personal Memory Vault," the ghost went on. "Please don't forget it next time you leave. It helps you relive your whole experience in here at home."

I ignored the gearbeasts, but the ghost kept following me. "Have you lost something?" it wanted to know. "May I help you? Just ask away!" as if it was a game Clusterhaunts liked to play. I wasn't here to talk, though.

There were just not that many alternatives. No wall panels to peel off the glass-like sides of the dome, no secret compartments embedded in the smooth, hard floor. The rubble under the fallen tail of the metal tube the ghost had called a rocket was a big pile of shards, and even the bases of the undamaged tables and cases were solid. So maybe talking *was* how I'd get to the heart of this ghost.

I turned very slowly. "You'd answer all my questions? Really?"

"Sure. That's what I'm here for." The ghost hovered expectantly.

I swallowed. I was a scout, not a master of eloquence. This could go horribly wrong. "Where is your heart?"

Among all the reactions I had anticipated, I surely hadn't expected the ghost's pronounced shoulders to sink. "Ah," it said in a somewhat small voice. "Well, you already saw on your first visit that I am not like you. And a heart is among the things that separate us." Its light grew dim. "Alas, I guess one could say my heart is up among the stars? That's where I always wanted to be, so maybe that's a justified notion."

So the ghost really liked its tall tales, liked them so much it spun its heart-concealing fabrications around them in a way that made me feel all wistful. I could have asked about its veins and lungs next, or any other part of ghost anatomy a good scout knew to look out for. But the only thing I seemed to remember was how it had tried to comfort me earlier, and somehow that made everything much more complicated.

It had diligently shuffled after me, and I was looking at its blurry form through a thin sheet of clear material mounted on a table between us. "What are you called, then?" I asked finally.

The ghost lifted its hand and dropped it again. "Oh, I . . . nobody ever calls me anything. I'm just here for your service. And on a better day, this should display the orbits of the main celestial bodies. It's in maintenance mode. I apologize for your inconvenience."

"Nonsense." I felt angry all of a sudden, and not just because I wasn't making any progress here, apart from trying to befriend a ghost. "People also don't call me anything since the Blessing came upon me. But I'm more than the service I render."

"I'm afraid that I am not."

I crossed my arms and hissed in frustration. Even those old gearbeasts had been named, however strangely. I could do better. "I'd like to call you Orion, then, if I may."

It just hovered there, frozen.

"I mean, we're not close enough for me to know your gender," I added. "So it's just a suggestion, yes?"

"It's a brilliant suggestion!" The ghost beamed, radiating brightness. "Orion . . . that's very considerate!"

I thought so myself. It was a name from the same old tales that told of the stars.

"Thank you, little explorer Mink. I'm attaching my name to all Memory Vaults now."

And in the newly brilliant light of Orion I saw something, off to the side. Something that shouldn't have been here, and yet there it was.

Inside one of the glass cases, bathed in wraithlight and completely still, sat a weaver.

"Don't touch the exhibit, please!"

I had taken the weaver out and set it on the floor, where it had very frustratingly not shown the slightest inclination to move. Clearly, it hadn't been able to bask in a long time.

"Little explorer. Your interest in this ATU shows how bright you are. But I counted 384 defects in here already, and you really shouldn't add . . . "

I gestured at the weaver. "What did you call that?"

"People call them space spiders, but officially it's an Advance Terraforming Unit." Orion drifted to another thin glass-like sheet, this one larger, mounted on the floor. "Come along! See them in action."

The weaver sat motionless. I would fetch this prize for my tribe, a new heirloom to complement our herds. But I also wanted to know how it had ended up in a glass case. Reluctantly, I followed the ghost.

"Still no music." Orion contemplated the large glass-like screen. "I'm sorry."

"I am sorry for adding another defect," I said, and I meant it. As much as Orion tried to make up for his failing contraptions with enthusiasm, I could still sense his distress. "Shall we sing again?"

I did not feel like it. I couldn't see any horizons manifesting themselves in my near future. I was still here to lay Orion to rest, the sooner the better. Had I stumbled upon him while advance-scouting, I would have turned my back and looked for another harvesting ground. But this was not an option with the tribe camping on the threshold, cultivating their superstitions.

"Maybe later, little explorer Mink. For now it will do, the display works just fine. Look."

At first, I saw nothing; nothing I hadn't seen before with minor ghosts. Ephemeral colors danced through the glass, almost too quick for the eye to follow. Then the whole screen, larger than myself, was filled with the image of a weaver. I sat on my haunches to get a better look. I understood now: Orion was showing me a vision.

"Moving mode; printing mode; charging mode," Orion said while the weaver flickered through a series of motions, completely translucent, so I could see its intricate inner workings. This was followed by an impossibly long line of weavers scuttling up a smooth ramp, then fire and smoke. "When the ATUs set out to terraform other worlds, they are equipped to deal with every hostile surrounding, to transform every unusual or even hazardous material into something useful," Orion said, and I slumped to the floor, curling my tail around my legs. "They are constructed semiautonomous, with modes to work on individual projects, to collaborate, or to be operated by a higher-level controller."

I must admit I wasn't able to follow his tale, but then I had never worked with a weaver, so what did I know? The images drew me in. Weavers glinting like gems in front of a profound blackness. Weavers swarming at structures I had never imagined. Weavers working away at something that looked like the dome I found myself in, but under two bright bluish suns.

"These are other worlds?" I asked. I saw them, but I couldn't believe they were real. New worlds, worlds not poisoned by a violent, unholy past.

Orion's head bobbed enthusiastically. "Yes, little explorer. There are many upon many, scattered among the stars. Everything you see in here, including the visitor center itself, was built to get there. Maybe you will travel to one of them yourself one day?"

I stood fascinated, watching, and I felt fear clamp down on my heart even as it soared. This, I knew, was ghost-shifting: ghosts telling about great things, about possibilities, about progress. It was not true, it just didn't happen, and when it happened, it was bad. This kind of thinking had destroyed the world. We were careful now, and we didn't pursue any stupid ideas.

But it was beautiful, and that had always been my weakness. I was transfixed by the images as they flickered by, bathing me in the brightness of distant suns. My gaze drank up the swarms of weavers spinning things far greater than we had ever dreamed of. And I realized they were so much more than what we had been using them for. This would be invaluable knowledge, if the tribe could accept it. I wondered if they would even accept a ghost-touched weaver, and resolved to tell them I had found it far from the place of the haunting.

I turned to look at the creature with renewed awe. But my colors flared in alarm at what I saw.

The first light of the day filtered in through the ceiling, and I realized I had lost the track of time over the ghost's stories. Several figures were clustered together near the entrance, shuffling and whispering. Among the dozens of weavers at their feet, the one marked white with dread-screen clearly stood out in the front row. Asper and his fellow herders had come to harvest. They craned their necks, staring at me. Staring at Orion.

"Visitors!" The ghost began to drift closer. "Are these your friends? More little explorers? I'd love to welcome them."

"No, Orion!" I tried to prevent what could only end in disaster. "Stay back, will you?"

The herders had already scattered. With hectic gestures they maneuvered their weavers to hide behind them, while some broke and ran for the entrance, shrilling a warning.

"Wait!" Asper yelled. "The Blessed is in the ghost's thrall. We have to rescue her! Get Renke, hurry!"

"It's alright." I made two steps towards them to show I was free to go. "He's nonaggressive."

It was a futile effort. Most of them were crazed with fear, clogging the narrow entrance tube or fleeing along the walls of the dome. Asper, though, not only came for me, but managed to bully a fellow herder to march with him towards much more ghost activity than any of them had ever seen.

"Asper, you have to watch this!" I backed off towards the glass-like screen. "We were all wrong about the weavers."

He grabbed my arm.

"Hey!" Orion drifted closer.

Without letting go, Asper jumped. I stumbled and was caught by his friend, who dragged me to my feet without any respect for shoulder joints and their natural resistance to jerking. I hissed.

"Hey!" Orion said, louder now. "I cannot tolerate violence in here. This is a place of peace and learning. Now, behave yourselves and release Mink!"

A collective gasp rippled through the herders as they heard the ghost speak my name, and I used their surprise to detach myself.

I could not let them take me. When they got me out of this dome, there would be no turning back and setting this right. Truss would die, unsung and alone, and I would not bring a new weaver and a new vision to the tribe. I tried to back away and babbled incoherent things that probably did nothing to convince them I was not ghost-shifted beyond repair. Orion's warnings became increasingly pressing.

When Renke's fighters joined the fray, they pushed the fleeing herders back in and moved towards me, crests rising as Orion drifted in between us as if to shield me.

Then, cutting through the very fabric of this old, untouched space, I saw the glint of a spear flying. Renke's verdigris green collar-feathers were tied to its shaft. It passed right through Orion, to bury itself in the screen containing the vision. A web of cracks appeared, and the light within died.

Orion's voice shrilled, distorted and much louder than before. "Stop damaging the equipment, and leave Mink alone, now! She's under my protection."

In the silence that followed, a rustling sound came up. It was a sound we knew, but it had a wrongness to it that made everyone freeze. Instead of the chaotic concert of individual clinks and whirrs, we heard our weavers march in unison. They came scuttling from all corners, flowing together like some big machine assembling itself. I knew this behavior, I had observed it moments before in the vision, but it was uncanny to see it executed, as if they had developed a shared, single-minded purpose all of a sudden. The others just stared, but some called out to their weavers, gesturing them back to no avail.

I froze when I saw what their purpose turned out to be. They all came up to me, smoothly parting around me and flowing into a new formation, climbing upon each other and surrounding me with a barrier of spiky metal.

And they were ready to defend. Asper and the other herders tried to intervene as the fighters tore into the formation, and they all got burned by spurts of heated material, seared by cutting-lights, sparks flying off their scales. They had absolutely no experience with the way the herds behaved now, like a single organism lashing out.

I tried to climb over my living protection, ready to leave with the tribe to end this. "Orion!" I cried. "Stop. Please!"

"Habitat security initiated, please cooperate."

"Orion?"

But he didn't respond to me anymore.

And I remembered the most important thing a scout has to recognize: the point when fighting would only lead to greater loss. I sounded the Rush. "Flee! This is a Clusterhaunt!"

Renke took up my tune, aggressively, urging on the herders who still called their weavers. I don't know what really made them break and run in the end. It could have been the herder who recognized the carapace of her weaver and tried to yank it out of the formation, only to get cut so badly we had to carry her. Limping and crying, we fled, and Asper's look was so hurt and betrayed I wanted to camouflage out of his sight. When I reached the entrance tube as part of the last group supporting and dragging each other, I thought I heard a faint whisper from the dome. "Safety can only be guaranteed in the habitat. Staying is recommended."

There was a difference I hadn't known, between separating myself from the tribe and being separated from the tribe. Oh, I was still with them, but I was kept off to the side, under guard. My status was unclear. Outcast, probably; a prisoner, surely; still useful, maybe.

Renke had screamed into my face, asking who would spin her a new spear, now that there was not a single weaver left. Asper had not spoken at all, but he surely cursed the day the tribe had acquired the clutch of supposedly blessed eggs that had hatched me. Others had said it aloud: "She who runs on her own shall no longer sing with us." And Truss had been loudest of all. "Is this how I taught you to serve your foster-tribe? You doom us all with your shrewd ideas. You shame me. You deny me my contribution to our survival, just because you're too sappy to accept what has to be done."

He might still get his chance to die all alone now.

My body's warmth seeped into the night-cooled ground. I was a miserable, pale heap, bound to a cracked column to protect everyone, including myself, from the mad bouts of my ghost-shifted mind. And as I stared up into the murky morning sky, still clear of the minor color shifts and scattered light that preceded a new wind, I knew they were right. I had been ghost-shifted. I had been blinded. The stars were not real. There was nothing but blackness up there.

I had been wrong all the time, dreaming of greatness and of knowing everything. I had chased visions and embraced change like it was just a pretty color I could wear, while secretly smiling at the superstition the herders held against me, never letting me approach a weaver. Now the weavers were taken, because I had lied. Because I had failed to see that they were right.

Not that anybody took the time to lay the blame at my feet—they would be crest-over-tails planning their next steps. I could hear them arguing. But it was just a waste of energy. Even if we stood a chance, we would never fight the one thing that let us thrive: our herds, our cleansers, our silvery lifeblood in this wrecked land.

Of course, without weavers, we would soon all be ghosts. And it would be a long drag down. We would wander the plains, deprived of our purpose, deprived of our calling and our sustenance. We hadn't needed the weavers to change the world, really, but as a reason to tread on, to lay claim to hostile territory, to sustain our foolish, desolate, stubborn way of living. We had never seen what they really were, until now that they were gone, and I was the only one . . .

No.

I had to give up this delusion. I had never been the only one. I knew nothing.

To the disgruntled huffing of my guard, I started a cleansing song. It was too late for that, but I had to do something to steer my mind from the tantalizing vision, from the dread and the despair.

When I heard the soft thud of footpads on the ground, I thought somebody might try to gag me. But next came a strangled sound from my guard while a weaverspun chain dug into her trachea; that made me jerk out of my song.

Under a cover of black fabric I recognized the loam-spotted greens of Asper's scales. My first thought was that he had come to personally punish me, and when he stepped closer, I expected him to tell me he wanted me gone, that he couldn't bear to feed me one more share of spicy mothfry after all I had done.

"They're gone, because of you. Poor Peshk needs a brace, because of you, and I can't build one, because of you." He stared down at me for a moment, his tail lashing. I cringed, which made him snarl even more. "What is it with you, crazy scout?" He took off his heat cloak and dropped it near the shadowed corner I was curled up in. "You're all sickly white."

I hooked the cloak with one claw and drew it to me cautiously. "It's . . . it's my mood, yes?"

"Then snap out of it! You'll need your skill after you've warmed up." He swallowed, as if the next thing he was going to say had a foul taste to it. "They are debating. But it all ends up the same—we're going to leave. Hoping to reach the settler townships and seek refuge there. They're packing already. We're abandoning our weavers." He took out a small trimming knife. "Can't let that happen. Can't just leave my Tineater serving this Clusterhaunt. So I figured you'd be the one to come up with another idea. I saw you talk to that ghost. Like it made sense. Maybe you're shifted, and surely you're as unclean as a cesspool full of ground poison, but you've got a knack for communicating with this thing." With one swift slash, he cut through my rope.

I didn't move, just sat numbly, completely baffled. And I wondered if everybody had this one breaking point that made them fall from grace. “This might not be in the tribe’s best interest,” I said softly. “What if I don’t come back and you’ll have to run without a scout?”

“Wrong time for regrets,” Asper snarled, and he sounded strangely like Truss to me, when he had taught a lesson. Then he tossed me my tools and turned around to sit next to the guard and check on her. “Go make some sweet talk to this ghost of yours, or rip its heart out. I don’t care. Just get Tineater back to me. Bring the weavers, or don’t come back at all.”

The moment I moved out of reach, he took up the cleansing song I had abandoned.

There were many reasonable things I could have wished for as I passed through the yawning portal into the dome again: that I knew a secret tune to make the weavers follow me out just like that; that I had Truss at my side, to hold me back with a sharp hiss from making yet another stupid mistake; that I could run, run the plains with my tribe and our herds whole and sound, and leave this place alone.

I might face the true power of the Clusterhaunt now, not the gentle inducements of the being I had dubbed Orion.

A name it hadn’t responded to any longer after it had turned on us. I was very much afraid that any bond Asper relied upon might have existed in my imagination only.

Foolish as I was, the thing I really wished for was that it hadn’t forgotten *my* name.

But Orion was nowhere to be seen. I could tell, because in plain daylight the murky darkness of the dome wasn’t absolute. High up, where some of its ceiling panels were missing, shafts of light sliced down all the way to the ground in cascades of dancing dust motes. And there was a flurry of ghost activity. Faintly blinking lights, ghostly chatter emanating from various objects, all clocked to the clinking and whirring of the weavers. It was every sane person’s nightmare, but I was beyond fear.

Or so I thought, because when Orion did descend upon me out of thin air, I blanched, flinched, and pinched my tail under a metal pedestal I knocked over while fighting for balance. Before I could lift it, two weavers scuttled over and hoisted it back up. I very slowly backed away.

“Little explorer Mink, adding some defects again, aren’t you? But don’t you worry. Mistakes happen, and I’ve got so much help now.” Orion drifted closer and lowered his voice. “We’re not officially reopened yet. You are a regular visitor, though. And I’m so glad to see you’re back, and unharmed, too, so I’m willing to make an exception. A special tour just for you, what do you say?”

Part of me wanted just that, to lose my unhinged, ghost-shifted self in visions. I swallowed. "Actually, I'm not here to visit you. I'm here for the weavers." I indicated three of the creatures, spinning upwards from the floor, thread after thread, grabbing shards with their long legs to absorb and fuel their weaving while building something that looked like it would go on top of the pedestal. "They don't belong in here. They are the herds of my tribe, you see, and we need them back."

"Weavers? You have a knack for names, little explorer Mink. But you must understand the ATUs are no playthings, and they are doing what they are made for. They are not mine to give back. But they do good work, and they are well cared for. Just imagine how many visitors will take delight in this place after all those pesky defects are behind us."

I took a deep breath. I very much detested breaking things. And it had been nice, nice to get to know someone who wasn't aware of the brokenness of the world, who didn't live under the constant pressure of survival. It had been nice, but it was the only leverage I had. "There is something you should know." I worked my jaw for a moment, like something old and awful was lodged between my teeth. "They are not coming. Nobody is coming. There are no visitors anymore."

"Little explorer!" Orion's gloved hand went up to his bowl-shaped head. "What are you saying? That's nonsense. Right?"

I came close to him, and I wished I could have reached up and taken the sides of the bowl in my hands, to look into those elusive eyes. And to have something to cling to, because it hurt, what I had to do. "It's true. Look at all those defects. And believe me, you got off lightly in here. The defects outside are numberless."

And I sung him the oldest parts of the Tribesong, the way the elders had sung it to me as a hatchling, lest I forgot how the world became broken and the reign of demons had ended when they choked on their own corrupted breath, after their insatiable thirst for knowledge had undone them.

When I sang no more, Orion was silent for a very long time. He didn't even hover or flicker. I tried to stay equally unmoved. The tribe, the herds, the running, hearts thumping up our chest. That was what mattered. Not a ghost and his grieving.

"I was built to teach," he stated finally, his voice unquavering and strong, and I thought that maybe his hidden lungs weren't built to produce the sobs buried underneath. "I was built to inspire new achievements. If it's all gone, and I'm all alone . . . why am I still here?"

I had no answer for him. Ghosts despised the living, that was why, and I knew that he did not.

Orion looked up again, a hint of eyes gleaming under the bowl. "But you. You will come? You, and your . . . tribe. You returned, after all. You want to learn."

I laughed. It sounded like choking. Learning was what had gotten me into this wretched situation in the first place. "No, Orion. We won't. I'm sorry. My tribe is fear-stricken by your presence. You have proven yourself a true Clusterhaunt by taking our weavers. You are the doom of my people."

"But everything will be fine in here soon," he insisted. "Zero defects. And you'll like the stars. I promise—"

"Orion. There are no stars." I had the distinct feeling that I was about to tear his heart out with words alone, and I had to speak around the lump in my throat. "The veiled moon is a silvery blotch gliding through the upper fumes. And the stars, they are gone so long they are not even in the Tribesong; a whisper of clear lights, shining through the dark fabric of the night to give us comfort. But we can't afford to believe in comfort. There is only blackness."

"Is that so?" Orion moved again, and this was the first time he tried to touch me. His fingers passed through my cheek, leaving faint traces of heat. "You should believe in comfort. It makes you reach out again after you fall. How else would you advance? When we set out to reach the stars, there were many who would have held us back. It's a risk, they said. A waste. But we sent our eyes up into the skies, and we saw worlds up there. We have always had to cross the blackness, Mink, and it has always been vast and intimidating. We have always fallen. But this place is a monument to our resilience, and it has seen visitors from afar, who brought back the evidence of those worlds. As its guardian, I was never intended to go myself, but I saw the blackness could be crossed. And you should have trust in that, too, Mink."

My mind went back to those pristine, luminous worlds of the vision, and there was comfort in the thought of them out there. I could not condemn this comfort, even if it made my heart want to reach out and find a way to get there. Even if I needed to embrace ghost-shifting to get only one step closer. And I did. "Show me."

He clasped his hands behind his back and nodded gravely. After a while, a weaver came scuttling out of the gloom to stand close to me and pinch me in the upper calf. In one of its legs, it held something, pressing it urgently into my hand as soon as I crouched. I looked at the smooth oval in my palm, then back at Orion.

"Your Memory Vault. I told you not to forget it next time you leave."

"I'm not leaving. I want you to show me your vision."

Orion shook his head. "No. Not only you. Bring your tribe. Let me show them. Only this one time. I am not your enemy. But this is the price I demand for giving back the weavers."

Never would the elders bring what was left of our tribe into the lair of the Clusterhaunt again. Never would they trust my word, ghost-shifted as I was. And yet. I wanted them to see. I wanted to be with them again, and that would never happen when my dreams lived among the stars, while theirs still had to cross the blackness. "I'll try, but my voice in the Tribesong is small."

"Nonsense" he said. "I heard you sing. There's nothing wrong with your voice. Just use it. Educate them."

He was right. They needed to know, and I had never made the effort to tell them anything. It had been easier for me, and easier for them, to carry on as we had always done. But there were other worlds, worlds not lost to corruption and poison. This was a vision as true as any prediction of our windreader. This was hope. It would be hard work, but I had to make them understand. Even if it meant breaking what was left of trust and love. Even if the only thing to speak in my favor was the prospect of a happy reunion with our herds.

Then Orion explained to me in detail how I would get the weavers back after the performance. If I hadn't believed him before, I would have done so now, because it was a sound plan. It was, in fact, a plan I had executed many times before. And as soon as I grasped what he wanted me to do, I threw up my hands and said: "No. I won't do that, Orion."

"But you must. As I said, the weavers are not mine to give back. When I initiated habitat security, they were integrated in the defense matrix. I can command them to repair while there is no threat, but I can't undo their integration. Security is automated."

I didn't understand, and I didn't care. I shook my head.

Orion waited very patiently by my side while I came up with other plans. Waited very patiently while I cried. And waited very patiently while I added one or three defects by kicking things.

But the world was less patient. It barged in on me when Asper crashed through the entrance, the fear in his voice overshadowed by the greater horror that must have driven him to brave the Clusterhaunt's lair yet again.

"Blessed!" he cried. "You have to lead us in the Rush, now! The camp was breached by a rustbreed vanguard. They have followed us."

We were nomads, and we didn't get to keep things. Not even dreams.

So I tried to shake it all off while I followed Asper into a nightmare. People were securing exhausted young ones to their chests or trying to force up the wounded, while right in the middle of the camp Renke and her fighters fell back against the rustbreed despite battling fiercely. Vanguard attacks were meant to delay and cripple until the arrival of the colony, and if they had to impale their sinuous bodies on our weapons to shower us in acids, they would do just that. Already the ground sizzled with ochre blood.

Everybody made way to let me take my place at the head of the column, to lead us on the quickest path out into the open, where we could outrun them. But my eyes searched for Truss' pallet, where he would die alone, as was his duty. And my mind went back to the dome, to my voice rising up through its stillness, stirring the dust of centuries.

I knew a safe place right under our noses. I could still get us out without anyone being left behind.

"No need to run," I told those nearest to me. "Bring your young ones into the dome. It's safe, I promise. The Clusterhaunt will protect us." They didn't move, of course, but I went on, louder now. "I bargained for our protection. Our weavers will defend us in the dome. You have seen what they are capable of! These walls are indestructible. It is our best and only chance! Go!"

Most of them muttered madness at me, but some snuck glances at the dome, leaving our formation with tentative steps. Others kept looking at the elders.

"Get back!" the windreader yelled, ushering them on. "Don't listen to this ghost-shifted rambling. We run!"

"But the Blessed is right!" I hadn't noticed Asper staying with me in the fray. He had leapt onto a crumbling wall, waving his heat cloak like a banner. "Our weavers are in there. I won't leave them. I say let's go and make a stand there! We've got nothing to lose."

I saw the eyes of the herders shift. Terrified, yes, but flecked with mad determination as they grabbed what they had dropped in the wake of the attack and started to run for the dome, a few first, but drawing more and more after them. And I saw Renke lose every battle she was in and buckle when she finally called her fighters to her side to cover our retreat.

And just like that, the tribe was on the move. I went to find Truss and lifted his dry, grunting weight upon my shoulders. He didn't quite struggle, but he did snarl.

"Don't you dare and deny me my choice. Leave me, and do what the tribe needs of you."

"I am," I snapped. "And you can thank me later, or still make use of your choice then."

He huffed, but sagged against me in defeat. The tribe had decided, after all. Just beyond the tube entrance, their courage left them, though, and they all stopped dead in their tracks. The space was brimming with ghost activity. "Orion!" I shouted, shouldering my way to the front, Truss still with me. "Where are you?"

"Mink!" The ghost blinked to life in all his silvery splendor between two shafts of light in the middle of the dome, making my people surge back against the walls. "I'm glad you came back! Come on, everything is prepared for the show."

"We're not here for the show. Please, Orion, you have to protect us. There's rustbreed at the threshold, and my people need shelter. Help us!"

The spear fighters defending the entrance shot frantic looks at Orion as he drifted closer, but the Warden called them back in line with a disdainful growl and motioned others to move up as replacements, should they fall.

"I see," Orion said, and my heart leapt when I felt his lighthearted nature yield to the gentle profoundness I had come to trust. "Harm to visitors is to be avoided at all costs. Initiating habitat sealing."

An inaudible command brought in our herds. From all directions, they converged upon the entrance, the staccato of clinking legs made it sound like we had acquired an army. Smoothly they flowed into precise lines, passing down chunks of material to the tube opening where the silvery creatures began to weave upwards from the ground, and downwards from the ceiling. Most herders just stared in astonishment, but some whooped and called their weavers' names, and a few ventured out to gather rubble for them. Not every fragment went into the quickly growing wall, though. Some ended up in scalding spurts directed at our enemies.

It was messy. Three weavers were thrown back in a spray of acid as they clung to the red-tipped mandibles of a rustbreed soldier to keep it from rearing. One of our fighters went down, hundreds of chitinous legs crawling over him. He was still screaming long after he had been pulled back out.

But soon there was only room left for a single rustbreed to squeeze through, and then not even that. The entrance was sealed, and we stood in silence, apart from the occasional thud when one of the creatures flung itself against the freshly spun concrete slab.

The tribe huddled together in the open space of the dome, eyeing me, the elders, and Orion. Some lowered the young ones to the floor, still holding their hands. Some flicked their tongues.

"What now, little foster-hatch?" I was kneeling next to Truss, trying to check his bandages. He slapped my hands away, but he was no longer bristling with fury, his crest drooping in concern instead. “Seems we are not to become rustbreed sustenance yet. But what do *we* eat? We don’t have a grub’s worth of food with us, and they won’t go away as long as their prey is so close.”

I looked up into the fearful faces of my tribe, who had trusted me in a way I would never have thought possible. “We have our weavers. And we have Orion. Surely there is something we can come up with.”

It took a long time to get them to talk. Half of them still believed the Clusterhaunt had set this as a trap for us, and they were unwilling to go near it. A few even snuck on their dread-screen, which they had brought with them of all things. Orion was no help either, curiously hovering close, displaying some tricks to get the attention of the young ones. The tribe had settled into an uneasy camp formation, a few lone bug-catcher lamps marking a perimeter, its guards clearly at a loss.

Those lamps gave us an idea at last. As soon as I had gotten the herders to talk not about our predicament or the implications of conversing with a Clusterhaunt, but about the glorious things their weavers could build together, they were unstoppable. Ideas flew back and forth, with Orion chiming in with detailed knowledge.

“These possibilities, Blessed . . . Mink!” Asper clasped my upper arm as if I weren’t the uncleanest being he had ever met. Still, I was not one of them. I had no clue what exactly they planned to build, but the gleam in Asper’s eyes told me it would be magnificent. “There is enough plastics in here to burn the whole colony to the ground!”

In our lamps, we used a burning paste spun from plastics. The weavers would tunnel deep and build some contraption to saturate the ground the rustbreed crawled upon and burrowed in, until all that was needed was a single spark, while we sat safely here in our indestructible dome.

“Of course you will have to learn to control the ATUs for this project, little engineers,” Orion told them. “I can’t do it for you.”

The herders were too agitated to notice, but his tone alerted me. There had been a calm finality in Orion’s words that suggested he was not planning to participate.

“Why not?” Asper asked. “I’d like to learn, but we are in a tight spot right now. I’d prefer to be educated when nothing tries to break in and eat me.”

“Nothing will breach these walls, little engineer. But you won’t be able to learn from me afterwards. There are rules, hard-coded rules I have to adhere to. I cannot order the ATUs to break down the interior of my visitor center to form flammable components. I cannot add defects. Habitat destruction is beyond my authorization.

As is sending the weavers out of the habitat to tunnel as long as they are integrated in the defense matrix. You have to take your weavers back. Mink knows how."

I jumped up from the resting place I had found when they had gone into technical details. "I told you no, Orion!"

The others looked at me in puzzlement. They didn't understand. I had not abandoned my old teacher, and I wouldn't abandon my new one, even if he had found better students now. The stabs of jealousy I had felt since Orion had begun to focus his enthusiasm on the herders subsided, though, when he took me to the side. "I can't give them back. So I need your help, and I'm very sorry for your inconvenience." He hovered closer, so close that for the first time I got a look beyond the bowl and saw more than just a hint of his eyes. They were bright and very blue, luminous like the worlds I had seen in his vision. "Mink. Most curious of explorers. You should know that nothing will change if you keep clinging to the long-forgotten remnants of the past. I don't belong here, and you know it. You opened my eyes to it. It would be a sad existence indeed to stay back with this knowledge, waiting forever. And I would have no one else lay me to rest."

"No! Laying to rest is for ghosts. You . . . are something else, Orion. I gave you a name. You showed me the worlds." I flicked my tongue, affectionately now, and in affect, because it passed through him yet again.

"Then save what's left of me." He drifted backwards, beckoning me to follow him. "Not these outdated projections, but what I stand for. This is my purpose after all, educating the next generation about becoming explorers, builders, spacefarers. Now go and save your tribe!"

He had led me to the gigantic metal tube, and pointed up its sleek form. Above its upper end, where it was still fastened to the ceiling, one of the dome segments was missing, big enough for a lithe scout to squeeze through.

I shook my head with closed eyes. Imagined one way it would all end, if I did nothing, and another, and another, all equally grim. When I finally buckled, I swallowed everything I wanted to say and turned to technicalities. "If I go, will there be enough time to teach them what they need to know?"

"They are quite adept already. They might have used high-tech tools to build spoons, but they are master-builders in their own way. I'll teach them everything they need to know about ATU coordination. I'll try to attend the process as long as I can, but as you know, residual energies are nothing but a short echo." He came closer, as if to take me in his insubstantial embrace. I wasn't entirely sure if I really felt his warmth or just imagined it. "I'm sorry you have to do this, to go into danger for me. But I'm glad you found me, I truly am, Mink. I'm glad I was not forever alone. Now don't you worry. Just remember, beyond the darkness, worlds are waiting."

What I saw when I climbed the rocket tube to the outside of the dome was a sea of writhing russet bodies. Rustbreed reek permeated the air, legs clattered like an upcoming storm. It made me understand, more than anything else, that there was no way for me to go back down and sit it out. To wait for another plan, a miracle, a change of rules, would have been madness. There was a hard-coded rule of the tribes: nobody survived a rustbreed colony. Vanguard, yes, even the first waves of the colony proper. But those below had already settled in, infesting the whole area. And yet I might be able to save everyone. Everyone alive, at least.

I looked down through the hole in the ceiling one last time. Even Asper still shied when Orion came close to point something out, and the others kept more than a healthy distance. They did not trust him like I did, but I hoped their shared passion for the weavers and Orion's attempts to entertain those who were not involved in building would keep the tribe from panicking.

I turned away and camouflaged. Everybody thought it easy, that I just had to press against any random surface and magically took on its color. But it's not like that. It is a process, a transformation, and it's more than scale-deep. The colors are a mental thing. My whole body wanted to scream danger in bright yellows and reds, and I had to convince it to calm down. When I felt positively invisible, I took up the rope and began my treacherous way down the side of the dome.

Even camouflaged, it was harrowing to see this dead place writhe with a host of centipedes prepared to tear me apart. After our first flight, there was not much left in my vial of extract from rustbreed scent glands, so I didn't fiddle with droplets, but threw the whole thing to shatter far from the place where they were clustered, obsessed with this frustratingly thin wall separating them from a tribe's worth of a feast. The whole ground seemed to ripple as they moved to investigate, and I was able to slip past the few remaining patrols.

I was possibly the very first scout to be led to a heart-chamber by the ghost's own words. It was located in one of the tall, broken buildings, beyond debris-strewn staircases descending far down into the bowels of the earth, into labyrinthine hallways with doors Orion had taught me to navigate. A true Clusterhaunt hideout, if there had ever been one. The entrance was signed in the way he had said it would, and I made short work of its grade-4 lock with a vial of potent acid. This was, after all, my trade.

I closed the door carefully behind me, then I looked around. And the moment I saw what this room was, my chest ached for Orion.

It was a cauldron of ghosts. It was a grave.

On its other end, massive vanes behind a metal grate streamed air into my face, sufficiently cool to immobilize anyone exhausted enough to give in to the cold. There were hearts aplenty, rack upon rack, neatly placed in their boxes. But only one was still beating.

"Orion." I stood transfixed by the slow pulses of light emanating from the box, placed my hand upon it like I had never been able to with his manifestation in the dome. Then I began to chant, because it was the only way to get moving again, to sink into the routine of a duty I had done so very often.

As I took down my tool sash and put on my gloves, I sang the Song of Passing, to tell the ghost that the sins of the past would be set right and there was no reason to linger, but I soon slipped into my own verses. I sang of the vastness of the fallen world and the vastness beyond, and I hoped it was bearable because he had my voice guiding him along. I sang of worlds beyond the blackness and a bowl full of stars, and I took my engraved pliers and plucked and cut at the right places, as gently as I could and with a touch that I hoped conveyed love, not violence, until the very last bluish light on the heart slowly faded.

A noise I had not perceived till now ground to a halt, and the breath of cool air on my face died. I let my own breath go in an anguished rush and slumped down on the lifeless heart-box, without a care for my unprotected face and arms.

At the afterthought of residual energies, I jerked up. Maybe there was still time for a proper farewell. I forcefully banned my grieving paleness and ran.

I came back to a darkened dome.

I knew what to anticipate: weavers under the control of our tribe again, flowing together to use up all the interior material of the visitor center to build secretly under the earth, slowly, but steadily creating the trap. The moment the weavers came together for their task, the rustbreed were dead already, their time burning down with every spun thread of tunnel, pipe, fuel, until they faced their immolation. I should have been glad to see the plan in motion.

Still, when I saw no ghostly lights shine from within the dome, my heart sank. I was too late. The last emanations of Orion had occurred without me. But then I heard the music.

Of all the things he could have repaired, of all the things he could have done with his last energies, he had chosen his beloved music. It was indeed very inspiring, swelling like the songs of a dozen tribes woven into one, ethereal, rising ever higher, tugging at the soul and then taking it along in a thunderous rush. The hexagons of the ceiling had been shaded to blackness, and I scampered down the metal tube of the rocket into a darkness speckled with the fearful eyes of my tribe under this display of ghostly power. Because there was also light.

Lights dotted the blackness. Clear and bright, beckoning, shining through the fabric of the artificial night. A few lone pinpoints first, then scattered scintillating clusters, until an abundance of lights pulsed above us. And as I came to stand among my people on the ground and let my gaze be drawn up, it was as if the domed ceiling had dissolved into an infinite, vast space, stretching out forever before our eyes, close enough to touch if we just strove to reach it.

None of us had ever seen the stars, but our hearts recognized them. They looked just like so many camps in the sky, bug-catcher lamps in the darkness, and I could not have been the only one to wonder what tribes lived up there.

Nobody made a sound, and only when the surging song Orion played for us ascended into our own Paean of Manifest Horizons did they move, like a collective sigh. And I could see that he had entered their hearts now, that he had become *our* ghost, with this last show, his star-laden farewell. Renke was studying their faces as well, and when she caught me looking, she simply nodded her acknowledgement.

And so when the weavers began to move, precisely coordinated, and when we began to hear the rustbreed blindly throwing themselves at the walls again, not knowing that even now their doom was in the making, and when the stars winked out in large swathes and it all went dark, our tribe sang on in the vast blackness, sang verses of new horizons and our ghost guiding us, and our voices filled the dome like an elegy, like a hymn, and took on a shape of their own, a shape of things to come.

When we set out to weave us a way to the stars, we knew we pledged the lives of our clutches to wandering the wastes. Generation after generation, we would scourge the ruins of the broken world for lost knowledge, our herds converging on molten glass seas to build miracles we had never dreamed of.

We are no mere survivors anymore. We are still adapting to our changed existence, as our starlit minds keep finding new paths in this old world. Our gaze is set upwards now, out to unpoisoned spheres, out to unveil the moon and what lies beyond. We will never be starless again, and this is the greatest gift, a glittering song to complement our own with hope.

When I walk the acrid sands with my ghost-shifted tribe, our two newly adopted gearbeasts trundling along, I know I will not be the one to actually bring us to the stars. This will fall to Asper, who teaches our future builders and planners to control their weavers, and to paint them, too, for beauty, not out of fear. My contribution to the Tribesong is small. But as I tell it once again, I'm clutching the Memory Vault, the only thing I took for myself from the visitor center that is now but an empty, scorched husk. They are like small eggs, those Memory Vaults. I'm not a fool. Most eggs come to nothing, I know. But maybe something will hatch. Maybe there is something left of Orion in there. I'll give it to the next scout after me, and she will give it to the next and the next until Orion's Song reaches the stars. Because as small as this contribution is, I know there will always be need of us who find new ways to cross the blackness and dream of the worlds beyond.

ABOUT THE AUTHOR

Simone Heller lives on an island in the river Danube in a town near Munich, Germany. As a literary translator, she lends her voice to writers in the sff field by day; by night she speculates on what-if questions in her own words. Obsessions include linguistics (in which she holds a master's degree) and cartography (in which she holds on to a collection of maps far more extensive than her wall space).

The Facecrafter

ANNA WU, TRANSLATED BY EMILY JIN

It was the end of all chaos.

The room was clouded with murky smog. Ling Xi had coughed herself awake.

She recognized the acidic smell of waste. *It's from the Agriculture Room*, she thought to herself, *the air pipes must have broken again.*

Rolling off her bed, Ling Xi began her simple washup routine. The stream of water dripping down the hose was even thinner than yesterday. Perhaps the rumors about the water storage system failure were not merely rumors, after all.

The face reflected in the mirror was so pale that it looked more like a two-dimensional figure, compressed to fit into the boundaries of a piece of print paper. In this gray container of barely ten square meters, her face was a grain of rice stuck to a sandpaper box.

Nuclear Winter had come for the humans ever since the end of the Great War. Lethal radiation dust snowed over every inch of land, leaving almost no bare ground. Humans were forced to migrate to the underground shelters built beneath the cities, where their habitable area was reduced to the minimum. Every shelter was divided into zones labeled as "agriculture," "pasture," "industry," "entertainment" and "storage." Clothing and food were distributed in uniform.

In some of those underground shelters, a small portion of the "storage" zone was left to preserve artworks. The city where Ling Xi lived was one of those cases.

In the beginning, those shelters were only designed to host humans for about ten years; yet in reality, the Nuclear Winter was much longer than what the scientists had predicted. The pollution caused by the new nuclear weapons was way beyond everyone's expectation. The hazy radiant dust gradually settled to the ground in six months' time, but the strong radiation persisted. Not a single plant could grow out of the damaged aboveground soil.

It had been a fleeting twenty years. Despite the fact that the shelters were constantly mended and converted, the lack of resources made it gradually more difficult to sustain the ecological system.

Ling Xi, an art major graduate, loved paintings. That was the reason why she chose to become the one and only "art keeper" of this city. The payment, in the form of cybercoin, was just as low as it could be; the only additional bonus was a tiny compartment with an even smaller window—this kind of room made up only one percent of the living compounds. The other upside of this job was the abundance of idle time.

Ling Xi pressed her face against the narrow window and looked down.

Thousands of residents in this city were leaving their capsules—their only living space—to gather at the few major roads. Together, they moved in the direction of the cafeteria, like a swarm of iron dust collecting around a giant magnet.

Breakfast would start in twenty minutes, but she had almost no appetite.

Three days ago, all of the paintings disappeared from the storage room overnight. The police investigation was deemed, however, fruitless: staff handover, the padlock, security videos . . . everything went precisely by the familiar routine, and there was absolutely nothing out of the ordinary.

It seemed like some magic made the paintings vanish into thin air.

Bewildered and clueless, the police had to drop the case.

But then again—in an era of underground shelters, who still cared for art? As soon as people managed to drag themselves through the long, laborious hours of work, all they wanted to do is seek refuge in the virtual world. The police, too, were not an exemption.

Ling Xi knew that her bosses would soon assign new work to her, but the very thought of how the artworks that she had guarded day and night with precious care were now in the possession of some thief still exasperated her. She could perhaps let it go if she knew that those paintings were in good hands—true, they were collecting dust and wasting away in the storage room anyways—but if they ended up ruined . . .

She couldn't bear to think more. A short stroll in "Eden"—the hottest global virtual entertainment community—should relieve her of these endless worries. She connected her brain to the cerebrum bridge equipment, and the familiar starting menu of "Eden" appeared at once.

"Have you had breakfast yet?"

Cang Jie's message popped up on her screen as soon as she logged online.

Interesting. She never remembered him as a talkative person. Why did he start the conversation first today?

Three months ago, she met Cang Jie online. The way he spoke gave her a gut feeling that he was a guy—well, she couldn't be entirely sure of it, because they had never met in reality.

At first, Ling Xi thought he was a writer, since "Cang Jie" was the name of the God who created language in ancient mythology. He was reluctant to talk about his career, however, so Ling Xi felt like it would seem too much like prying if she asked more questions. They grew friendly very fast, when Ling Xi realized that he was also deeply fascinated by the aesthetics of dance and art history. They had never met each other "in person," though—not even through each other's online avatars. All of their conversations took place on the chatting software. Ling Xi was not a fan of online avatars; for the same reason, she had never commissioned any Facecrafters to design one for her. Cang Jie never suggested that they should meet up in "Eden" either, anyways.

It seemed like they were both the outliers of this world.

"Nope."

"Go eat something. It will be a stressful day."

"What stress? Remember what I told you yesterday? I practically lost my job—damn the thief!"

Cang Jie hesitated, and then sent her a crying emoji.

"Isn't this thief absolutely sick?" Ling Xi continued to vent.

Cang Jie was silent for an entire minute, then his profile picture darkened suddenly, showing that he had just logged off.

What is this nonsense?

She desperately needed to cheer herself up. Maybe something in "Eden" would do the work.

In the virtual world before Ling Xi's eyes, various different countries and eras were all up for selection—nowadays, virtual worldbuilding was unquestionably the top most thriving economic industry.

The "Prehistoric" zone was bustling with people. That new Zhu Lu Boy Band was probably performing again. Just as Ling Xi wondered whether she should stop by as well, her visual sensor suddenly blacked out.

She immediately reached for the emergency exit button behind her ear, thinking it was an equipment failure.

Nothing happened.

When her vision was finally restored, she suddenly found herself in an all-too-familiar place—the Art Storage Room.

Weird . . . had this place been added to the virtual server too?

The security system scanned Ling Xi's pupils and the door in front of her opened. The overhead light flickered once or twice before finally casting a dim glow onto the room.

Everything here was exactly like the real world, even down to details like the room temperature—it was always colder in the storage room. Ling Xi wrapped her cloak tightly around her body. The winter clothes she usually wore in "Eden" had somehow disappeared, she noticed, and instead she was wearing her work uniform from the real world: a thin, almost shabby-looking gray cloak. The machine in the clothing factory had broken down a while ago; not only did nobody know how to fix it, the humans had no resources or storage capacity to produce extra clothes, either.

The government always said that the average temperature control in the underground shelters was around 15 degrees Celsius for this winter, but Ling Xi was almost certain that the real number was much lower than that.

She trudged slowly in the narrow aisle, passing by rows and rows of cabinets that glistened with a cold, metallic spark, her footsteps echoing in this enormous empty space.

Randomly, she pulled open a cabinet door, and found that the lost paintings were still in there, safe and sound. Perhaps this virtual scene was made before the burglary and hadn't been updated since then.

Ling Xi suddenly halted as she passed by a storage area. One by one, the cabinets in front of her creaked open, as if an invisible hand was controlling them. She could see, however, that three of them were empty.

Knowing the storage room catalog like knowing her own mind, Ling Xi identified the missing pieces immediately: *Les Demoiselles d'Avignon. La Muse. Guernica.*

She frowned. All three of the missing paintings were from Picasso—classic works of Cubism. Why? She shut the cabinet doors closed and looked up.

A rectangular black void around the height of an adult had appeared just a few steps before her, floating about ten centimeters aboveground. Ling Xi circled around the void. The void looked like it was as thin as a piece of paper; a two-dimensional construction inserted by force into a three-dimensional world. It reminded Ling Xi of the time traveling wormhole from *Doraemon*, one of the most popular animated shows of the past era.

She instinctively tried to touch it, but then decided that it would be too risky. Instead, she pulled out her smartphone to scan the void with her camera lens, thinking that she might find some additional information.

Unknown texture. Calculating length on width gives the perfect golden ratio.

A white silhouette emerged from the black void. Gradually, the figure grew larger and larger, as if they were walking towards the exit of a dark, deep tunnel. As they reached the opening of the void, they bowed their head slightly, and then tapped the ground with a foot as if they were gracefully descending an invisible stair.

Ling Xi found herself uncontrollably backing away. Accustomed to the abundance of horror games in the virtual world, she thought she was used to seeing strange things already, but this figure still sent a chill down her spine.

The figure was around 1.9 meters of height, their body wrapped loosely in a white robe of unknown texture. Black, silky hair drooped all the way down to their waist like a waterfall.

They wore an oval-shaped, white waxen mask. The mask, almost entirely empty, depicted no facial features save for a pair of thin, dark eyebrows.

Androgynous, every line and curve carved to perfection—the mysterious figure was just like a beautifully crafted idol.

They waved their hand. A gray cabinet opened automatically, and a painting inside—Ling Xi recognized that it was Picasso's *Dream*—rose slowly into the air.

A second painting followed immediately after, and then a third, a fourth . . . not a single piece of art was spared. The empty storage cabinets hung open like hundreds of gaping mouths.

Stunned, Ling Xi stood and watched. All of the art and calligraphy works floating midair began to converge, soon amalgamating into a massive, colorful collage.

Then, the figure glided toward her, as elegant as if dancing to some muted tempo. In the dim, dreamy light, with their robe rippling in the wind, they looked just like a phantom.

"Hun Dun."

The name was like a streak of lightning that ripped through Ling Xi's foggy mind. In horror, Ling Xi realized that this person must be *that* Facecrafter who had never appeared in front of the world before. From what she could recall, Hun Dun was their name.

Slowly, Hun Dun walked towards her. They smelled as fresh and cold as a river breeze.

" . . . An era where moral is corrupted, art is ruined, and talent has gone unnoticed like great pearls veiled in dust." They murmured coolly, their voice faint and low.

They lifted their hands and drew intricate lines with pale, slender fingers, as if they were pulling some invisible cords.

The giant collage started to spin, changing form rapidly as it rotated: from a two-dimensional image into a three-dimensional cube, then spreading out to form a kaleidoscopic fantasia. It was as if thousands of different angles and perspectives of gazing at the same collage had been magically squeezed into the same dimension and fused together.

Finally, the transformation came to a halt. Before Ling Xi's eyes hung a hypercube consisting of so many different shapes and colors that it was almost utterly indescribable. It immediately stirred up a strong feeling of nausea in her—the image was almost too dense and too complex for her brain to even begin to process.

As the hypercube emerged, Hun Dun was changing shape as well. Their masked face slowly melted into a swirl. The swirl was just like the empty drain hole in a swimming pool after the stopper plug had been removed, or a magnetic, bottomless black hole: it began to consume the hypercube, transforming it into liquid and then sucking it in.

A roaring river of colors rushed past Ling Xi, flowing so fast and ferocious that it nearly knocked her over.

All of a sudden, Hun Dun extended their left hand towards Ling Xi and tapped her lightly on the forehead. Their fingertip was as cold as the ice from an ancient glacier.

"The Day is near, only lingxi[1] can save it."

Ling Xi blacked out at once.

The next day, Ling Xi went to the hospital.

The hospital was shabby, and barely any working staff was around. Ling Xi glanced at one of the wards. Despite the fact that it was still working hours, a doctor and a few nurses, dressed in crumpled uniforms, were sprawled across a few sickbeds. All of them were connected to the cerebrum bridge. They resembled exactly what one would expect of the people living in this era: wan, skin-and-bones, crooked, sluggish, lips curled into a dazed smile.

At this moment, what kind of alternative lives were they leading in the virtual world? Aristocrats? Upper class socialites? Olympic champions? Master politicians? Were they enjoying the most extravagant dance performances, or were they savoring the taste of the most exquisite cuisine?

It all depended on how much they were willing to spend. Commissioning a decent Facecrafter and purchasing scenario backdrops could be worth quite a lot.

After gaping at those zombie-like creatures for a few seconds, Ling Xi continued down the corridor until she reached the room where her brother Ling Bai stayed.

Leaning against the pillow, a very pale Ling Bai was struggling to eat the food that his sister brought for him. It was the standardized menu from the cafeteria—steamed potatoes, stir-fried seaweed, vitamin water, and a hard-boiled egg that Ling Xi had paid an astronomical figure for to obtain on the black market. He had grown so unfamiliar with the texture of hard-boiled eggs that he almost choked himself on the egg yolk, and he burst into a fit of coughs.

Yesterday, after pulling an all-nighter to work, he fainted in the lab out of hunger. His colleagues discovered him this morning and sent him to the hospital immediately. *He probably spent all his money on the black market again to buy new materials for his experiments,* thought Ling Xi.

Ling Bai majored in Genetic Engineering, and he worked for the Agricultural Research Center. Everyone thought of him as a hopelessly romantic science nerd, who had been obsessed with a kind of purple colored plant that resembled the shape of a dog's tail. The plant's scientific name was *Purpureus Herba*, but both Ling Bai and Ling Xi called it "the dogtail grass."

According to years' worth of research, Ling Bai firmly believed that the only way to save humankind before the underground shelters fail was to breed organisms that could degrade the radiation on Earth's surface. However, his work on artificially synthesizing the DNA of *Purpureus Herba* had hit a plateau—the failure rate was stuck somewhere around ninety-five percent. At this pace, the Agricultural Research Center would soon revoke all the funding allocated to this project.

When humans first entered the era of underground shelters, they had exhausted almost every available way to save humankind from destruction, yet the Great War did not leave Earthlings with many resources to spare. The kindling of hope for a better future was thus quenched by thousands of failures.

"Our office's budget was cut down by half again. The money was allocated to the computer engineers. They say that those people need to create a new facecrafting program. Well, it sure is the only thing that can bring any profit nowadays." Ling Bai appeared visibly upset.

Ling Xi planned to threaten her brother that she is going to let him starve to death the next time she catches him overworking himself, but upon seeing his face, she swallowed back her words again.

Ling Bai pulled out a small test tube from his pocket and gazed lovingly at a fuzzy, purple plant inside. "Dogtail grass is far more important. Humans are such myopic animals!"

"Well, what your face looks like is important too . . . see, you just don't understand . . . look at how handsome the Zhu Lu Boy Band is!"

Ling Bai snorted. "Zhu Lu? What kind of oh-so-chic Facecrafter made this one, then? Everyone's face looks as if they came out of the same produce line! Doesn't anyone ever get tired of them?"

"I didn't actually pay that much attention—you know that I don't follow these things—but I heard that Zhu Lu made their way into the top three months after their debut. Their dances are very special, too—they do things like monsters and mythologies, battle between the Gods and all that. They are nothing like those corny and lame bands. The facecrafter who made them must be an expert."

Ling Bai looked crestfallen. "Now everyone's watching the Gods, no one cares about grass anymore!" He sighed. His eyes were still fixated on the test tube.

After a moment of hesitation, Ling Xi decided to tell her brother about what she saw in the virtual world yesterday.

Blacking out and seeing illusions in the virtual world could be taken either just as a joke or very seriously. There had been several cases of sudden deaths in the virtual world, as well.

"As far as I know, there has never been a scenario modeled after a storage room in the virtual system. What happened to you can only be explained by a system error or a pons failure, resulting in an illusion. Are you sure that you feel fine?"

Ling Bai's rounded face looked paler now. He gave his sister's shoulder a tight little squeeze, as if to make sure that she wasn't just an illusion, too. After their parents passed away, they were each other's only family left.

"Yes, I feel fine, but this is exactly what makes it weird. Vomiting, arrhythmia, fever . . . none of these typical side effects of pons failure has happened on me. Are you sure there isn't a different explanation?"

"Such as?"

"Is it possible that the masked person in white is the thief who stole the paintings?"

"But why would a thief want to give you hints? Isn't that just walking straight into a trap? I think you're just imagining things because you can't get over those paintings."

"Everything I saw was too real to be illusions."

Ling Bai pouted at her as if he was coaxing a child. "Ok, keep talking."

"First of all, in reality, all the paintings disappeared together; but in the virtual world, the three paintings by Picasso disappeared first. Why? Those three paintings are connected by a common trait—they are all works of Cubism. What does this signify?"

"Cubism?"

Ling Xi inhaled deeply. "Cubism . . . in short, it means that Picasso cuts up a three-dimensional space into fragments, reorders them, and then pieces them together to produce a collage of some sort. As a result, although he technically creates two-dimensional paintings, those paintings are actually depictions of the different perspectives of three-dimensional spaces."

She found a picture of *La Muse* on her smartphone. In the center of the painting was a woman. Half of her face was depicted through a frontal view, while the other half was depicted through a side view.

"Look, in this painting, Picasso takes two different perspectives of the woman's face and fuses them together to create the most unique image. His minimalistic style and bold strokes help draw the viewers' attention to the woman's face, too." Ling Xi gazed at the picture admiringly.

Ling Bai frowned. His eyes narrowed, indicating that Ling Xi's words had elicited some sparks of interest in him. "A three-dimensional world portrayed through shifting, alternative perspectives . . . what if the paintings are not portraying a three-dimensional world, after all? They could very well be creative attempts at displaying what a four-dimensional world would look like."

"Are you saying that Picasso has found a way to depict the higher dimensions?"

"Yes . . . wait, tell me more about the octachoron you saw in the illusion."

"Octachoron?"

"The hypercube."

Ling Xi described to Ling Bai again the scene she had witnessed in the virtual storage room.

"First, the paintings were pieced together into a collage—two-dimensional; then, the collage started to spin and gradually transformed into a cube—three-dimensional. As for the hypercube, I have a feeling that it is a four-dimensional figure. The reason you find it so strange and volatile, is because it is merely the projection of a four-dimensional object in a three-dimensional space."

"Projection?"

"In other words, if we compare the three-dimensional world that we live in to a piece of paper, all we can see of the four-dimensional hypercube is the part of it that comes into contact with the paper. As the hypercube rotates, its contact with the paper will change form as well. We cannot even try to predict the pattern of the transformation, since we are unable to imagine what the hypercube—as a four-dimensional object—would look like, just like how it would be almost impossible for a two-dimensional figure drawn on a piece of paper to imagine what our three-dimensional world would look like.

"If this thief can control objects in a four-dimensional space, then they must have come from higher dimensions—perhaps five, or even more. For them, extracting items from a world of lower dimension should be no more than a piece of cake, no matter how strict the security is."

Excited, Ling Bai reached for a piece of paper and traced out the shape of a man. Then, he drew a tiny little heart for the doodle man.

He poked at the heart with his finger. "Look, even though this two-dimensional figure's body is a perfectly enclosed oval, I can still get to its heart without breaking apart the line that makes up its body."

"You mean, despite that the storage cabinets were sealed, the thief was still able to remove all the artworks, because they did it from a higher dimension?"

"Yeah!" Ling Bai pounded his fist on the table. "The hypercube is a hint left for you—it means that you should consider the problem from a perspective of higher dimension!"

"To portray the three-dimensional world in which humans live through a two-dimensional painting is already an art of dimensionality reduction. An ordinary painter can only convert between the third and the second dimension; but for the great masters, they are able to depict not only three, but even more dimensions through art . . . " Wondered Ling Bai.

Ling Xi rose to her feet. Slowly, she made her way to the window. "A while ago, I saw some time-lapse photos taken of the starry night in reality. The shape and color of the distorted starry night look incredibly similar to that of Van Gogh's painting, *The Starry Night*, from hundreds of years ago. If we see Picasso as a painter of space, then Van Gogh should be . . . "

"A painter of time."

Lost in thought, Ling Bai gazed intently at the tiny plant inside the test tube and muttered. "The ability to navigate between dimensions . . . these great Masters of Art can see the world in a way that we cannot."

• • •

Cang Jie disappeared for three days. Ling Xi spammed his inbox with messages, asking him what he had meant the other day about "a stressful day," but he never came online.

Finally, on the morning of the fourth day, Ling Xi received a message from him.

"In ancient Chinese mythology, Hun Dun, Tao Tie, Tao Wu and Qiong Qi were recognized as the four guardian beasts. As recorded in *The Classic of Mountains and Seas*, Hun Dun usually appears as a slender, androgynous, faceless figure, consistently seen in a white robe. They are known for their talent and appreciation for art, especially dance and music. They are also exceptionally skilled in accumulating wealth.

"Putting aside the legends, however, the true form of Hun Dun is the God of Art and Beauty. As a deity, they live in a higher-dimensional space that is far beyond human comprehension. Throughout the history of Earth, Hun Dun has appeared as a part of different centuries and different cultures under altering forms of disguise. For example, in ancient China, Hun Dun was seen as a mythical guardian beast; in ancient Greece, on the other hand, Hun Dun was referred to by the name Venus. During eras when the arts and aesthetics flourish, Hun Dun hides behind the scenes; however, when moral becomes corrupted and art becomes neglected, Hun Dun will most definitely appear on Earth, in one way or another, to intervene."

Ling Xi did a cross-check between the information that Cang Jie had sent her and her own research. The first half about *The Classic of Mountains and Seas* still made some sense, but the second half seemed more like a terrible joke than anything else.

Her initial reaction was to immediately type out several pressing questions in the chatbox for Cang Jie to answer, but after a long hesitation, she replaced the lengthy paragraph with only three words:

"Who are you?"

Cang Jie, however, avoided her question.

"Hun Dun is my teacher."

"Is Hun Dun a Facecrafter?"

"Yes."

"No wonder you were upset when I called them a thief. Are you a real person, then?"

In response, Cang Jie threw another question at her instead.

"Does my teacher remind you and your brother of anything?"

"What do you mean?"

"I mean . . . I mean his research."

"His research? Isn't his research all about the dogtail grass? What are we supposed to be reminded of?"

"I can't tell you more, or else it will begin to affect the course of history. My teacher asked me to give you two electronic tickets. A show is coming up in three days. Remember to come see it."

"What does 'The Day is near, only lingxi can save it' mean? The Day for what?"

"Have you ever heard of the story of the Great Flood?"

"What are you even talking about?"

"It won't be the first time, and it won't be the last time either."

Cang Jie's profile picture darkened almost instantaneously after making this comment, showing that he had logged offline. Ling Xi, not wanting to give up just yet, furiously typed out more questions, but he responded no more.

Hun Dun, the God of Art and Beauty, Cang Jie, brother, The Great Flood . . . Ling Xi began her research with a series of keywords.

The Bible . . . the story about The Great Flood . . . to punish the misdeeds of humans, God sent The Great Flood. The flood persisted for forty days and forty nights. Every living creature—birds, animals, insects, and of course all the humans—died from it.

Then she browsed the wealth ranking of all the Facecrafters in the country. Although she had already expected this, she still couldn't help herself from gaping at the number of digits in Hun Dun's income—undoubtedly, ranked number one on the list.

There was also a demonstration of Hun Dun's previous works, all of which were virtual avatars in different shapes and forms, each with a unique touch. Fan comments followed after: "bringing artwork to life," "strokes of genius," "like nature itself . . . "

Hun Dun is exceptionally talented in accumulating wealth . . . but why would the cybercoin we use in this world matter to them, anyways? Why would they want to destroy humankind? If they really were a deity, why did they disguise themselves as a Facecrafter? Ling Xi wondered.

Facecrafter was a word that first appeared a century ago in computer games. It was meant to describe the creators of virtual avatars. In the beginning, restrained by technology, facecrafting was relatively simple. However, the arrival of the "underground shelter era" caused all-immersive virtual reality technology to come to an exponential bloom—the bleakness of the real world gave the people no choice but to seek joy in a virtual world.

Facecrafting, now an independent career, was also consequently recognized as an art instead of a simple handiwork. Expert Facecrafters would even buy or develop software of their own just to craft virtual avatars, collect face templates of the known beauties from history, and analyze them relentlessly. These days, a well-made avatar could be worth an entire city.

"The Zhu Lu Twelve," a boy band of twelve virtual characters, was Hun Dun's finest masterpiece. With every character created by Hun Dun singlehandedly, Zhu Lu was, without any doubt, the jewel of the crown. Three months ago, they made their first debut on stage in the online community. Since then, all of their concerts had been swarming with spectators, consequently bringing Hun Dun an enormous fortune.

Ling Xi sent a video chat request to Ling Bai. Ling Bai accepted the request quickly, yet he contemplated for a long time before finally opening his mouth, his face stern and gloomy.

"First of all, assuming that what you saw the other day in the virtual storage space was real, then we are facing a matter of grave consequence. If Hun Dun really is a deity who comes from a world of higher dimension, then from their perspective, humans are practically helpless. See, humans started the nuclear war, and now they are bounded in this morbid state, cooped up in underground cells to escape from the consequence. Humans have shoved aside the artworks that represent thousands of years of wisdom and left them to rot; humans have forgotten, too, their ambition a century ago to change lives through technology. All they care about now is the fake excitement that the virtual world could bring them. They can squander away millions of cybercoin for the artificial, so-called 'beauty,' yet they can't even stand to look at a Picasso for longer than five minutes. Isn't this exactly what Hun Dun was talking about? 'An era where moral is corrupted, art is ruined, and talent has gone unnoticed like great pearls veiled in dust.'"

"Is Hun Dun really going to destroy the world with a flood?"

"Don't forget that Hun Dun is an organism from a higher dimension. Maybe they are only trying to give us hints through ways that we can understand. As for destroying the world, Hun Dun doesn't necessarily have to do it through a flood; moreover, the destruction could very well be targeting only humans, while sparing all the other creatures. Remember what Cang Jie said? 'It won't be the first time, and it won't be the last time either.' Think about all the civilizations that have been destroyed: Loulan, the Mayans . . . "

"Even the dinosaurs?"

"Maybe. But Cang Jie said that Hun Dun's plan is related to my job . . . also, Hun Dun said something about 'only lingxi can save it.' I think they might be hinting at a way to redress this."

"Does this Facecrafter want to save humankind or destroy humankind?"

"There's something else that I heard about. I'm sure similar news has gotten to you as well. They say that the underground shelters can't hold up anymore . . . a friend who works for the government showed me some data. At maximum, the rest of the energy can only last us a few more months. Perhaps, with or without the Hun Dun's intervention, we will be facing destruction regardless."

"What should we do then?"

"I don't know. Okay, I need to go think some more about the dogtail grass. You should try to pry some more information out of Cang Jie."

Ling Xi didn't know what to do. Her instinct told her to trust what Ling Bai had said, yet her logic still protested against this absurd assumption.

"Stay strong. Anything can happen in this universe." Said Ling Bai before he hung up the phone.

Next day was Zhu Lu's last performance.

Over the past few days, Ling Xi had read all the information on Zhu Lu that she could find.

Realistically speaking, the boys of Zhu Lu were not even close to what you would call "beautiful" in the terms of the modern society. The most popular online avatars were modeled after perfection: broad shoulders; long, lean legs; skin as smooth as silk; delicate facial features that strictly followed the golden ratio. They were the angels roaming in a digital Garden of Eden.

But Hun Dun's creations were almost the exact opposite. The members of Zhu Lu were nowhere near perfection: some had short, stout legs and a bushy beard; some had noses too large or eyes too small. Yet, oddly, the twelve avatars of Zhu Lu possessed a fierce and raw kind of vitality that distinguished them from all the other virtual icons.

As soon as Ling Xi saw them, she immediately understood why Hun Dun was such a successful Facecrafter—the sheer power of Hun Dun's artwork was enough to breathe life into artificial creations.

The smoothness and cleanness of their choreography also far exceeded that of every other virtual performance troop. Many experts had tried to analyze the data modeling of Zhu Lu, yet they discovered that the algorithm of Zhu Lu was so complex and advanced that it was far beyond what they could comprehend. No one could figure out the true identity of this mysterious Facecrafter.

Furthermore, Hun Dun's choreography mostly took inspiration from ancient Chinese culture, where he uniquely combined classical

Chinese elements with other art traditions from around the world. Ling Xi remembered seeing some similarities between Zhu Lu's dance moves and the figures depicted by ancient pottery or bronze artifacts.

For the act titled *Nirvana*, the performers' masks had long ears, high nose bridges, sunken eyes, and foreheads with sharp edges, very much resembling the Easter Island statues. In the end, a mysterious fireball shooting across the sky crashed into the ground. In a ring of flames, the souls of the people ascended into the vast, dark space.

For the act titled *Flying Apsaras*, the performers were dressed up as the figures represented in the Dunhuang frescoes, playing four-stringed lutes and bamboo flutes as they danced gracefully in colorful robes. As soon as a pack of beasts with bronzed skin appeared on stage, the beautiful melody suddenly became the most powerful weapon: each musical note materialized into a dagger that dashed towards the beast pack, engaging with them in a battle.

The more Ling Xi watched, the more her heart sank.

The choreography, use of color, and sheer imagination of this performance seemed way too perfect—perfect to the point that they were almost unnerving.

The next act came up, and Ling Xi saw that Cang Jie was the protagonist.

The act was titled *The Creation of Written Language*. This was the first time that Ling Xi had ever "seen" him. He looked no older than a teenage boy, and his features resembled people from the prehistoric period. He had a bronze complexion, broad thick shoulders, and very distinctive facial features. The distance between his eyes was slightly too wide, but this characteristic only enhanced his boyish robustness.

The most special feature about his face, however, was his eyes. Each of his eyes had two adjacent pupils, as if they were the moon and the moon's reflection in a pond.

On the screen, Cang Jie led the dance as other performers followed. Just as Ling Xi watched, Cang Jie messaged her all of a sudden.

Can we meet in "Eden"?

As if she had been caught red-handed in crime, a pang of panic and embarrassment arose in Ling Xi, almost making her fall off her chair.

. . . Sure.

Cang Jie sent her the link to a personal virtual space.

Ling Xi connected to the cerebrum bridge, and a thick fog swallowed her at once. When it cleared up again, she found herself before a graveyard. Rows and rows of erected tombstones were veiled in a thin, white mist, looking almost as if they were floating amongst the clouds.

She could smell the familiar scent of ink, but her gut told her that something was wrong. Every once in a while she practiced calligraphy too—the ink scent that she usually smelled was alive, with a sharp, fresh hint of wood and grass, yet the ink here smelled moist, rotten and lifeless. For this reason, she almost resented the place immediately.

Cang Jie was waiting for her at the entrance to the graveyard. An amber light shimmered in his odd but beautiful double pupils. He scratched his freckled, round nose. He wore a cloak made from turtle shells that were connected together by thousands of tiny knots and tassels. As he moved, the knots and tassels bounced against each other, creating a rustle.

Ling Xi had never seen any avatar in the virtual world so well-crafted that their facial expressions and actions were as fluent and vivid as humans. In fact, the boy before her eyes looked even more real than any living human.

"Uh . . . sorry about this. I know it's a bit scary here. My teacher crafted this scene . . . he always likes to speak of things such as 'the written language is dead' . . . a lot of times, he is just like a little child. It bothers him, too, the way that you guys are treating this world, you know?"

"Does he mean to kill us, or save us?" Ling Xi asked.

"Well, there's no need to activate 'Operation Wipe Out' yet . . . you know that the underground shelters won't make it much longer, right? Also, my teacher isn't actually in charge of wiping things out—other Gods will do the job. Maya was a product of 'Operation Wipe Out.' I wasn't there to witness what happened, though, because my teacher hadn't created me yet back then . . . I heard it's because the Mayans were destroying the ecological environment . . . "

The phrase *wipe out* sent a shiver through Ling Xi's body.

"Teacher was angry upon seeing how those artworks were neglected. He was going to take them all away and leave you humans to face the destruction alone . . . then, when he saw the effects that Zhu Lu had on you lot, he changed his mind again . . . " Stammered Cang Jie.

"Can you help us?" Ling Xi grasped one of Cang Jie's sleeves. The small knots and tassels on his cloak rustled again.

Cang Jie blushed. "No, Teacher's authority isn't enough to intervene directly . . . there are other Gods in charge, too! Just think about the first time you saw Teacher. There will be more hints at the performance tomorrow."

He glanced at her with a stern look in his eyes. "Ling Xi, tomorrow—tomorrow is your last chance. We are leaving with Teacher immediately after the performance. Do you understand?"

Ling Xi was utterly out of words.

Cang Jie's figure gradually faded out. For no reason, Ling Xi felt like she saw a shimmer of sadness in the boy's eyes before he had vanished entirely. His personal virtual space, too, disappeared into a void of darkness.

Midnight was close.

Ling Xi and Ling Bai took their seats in the largest Central Theater of "Eden." It was a full house—understandably, though, since tonight was Zhu Lu's last performance before their retirement. Allegedly, a ticket to this performance was worth an astronomical amount of money on the black market.

Ling Xi glanced at her brother and managed to stifle a giggle. Both of them had to choose a virtual avatar tonight for the performance. Amongst the free avatar templates, he had chosen a narrow, sculpted face. Perhaps it was because his face in real life had always been plump and round. As for Ling Xi, she chose one of the free "beauty faces" as well. Her face was very roughly made and had been solely designed to match the standardized criteria.

Ling Bai grasped the dogtail grass test tube tightly. He had been unusually quiet for the night.

The theater darkened. The audience went silence at once.

First came the smell of brooks and rivers, drifting on a gentle breeze. Then a light shone, illuminating the stage. There was a great river in the center of the stage, its water murky and yellow from mud. Amidst the roaring waves, stood a figure in a white robe.

Only Ling Xi and Ling Bai recognized the figure. It was their first—and perhaps last—appearance in a performance.

Burying their face in their palm, Hun Dun sobbed. The water rose to their waist, tinting their white robe the same dingy yellow. The ends of their dark, long hair flowed with the current. They ripped at the edge of the mask, half-lifting it up, as if they wanted to tear it off completely. Blood and tears gushed from the crack and trickled down drop by drop, each drop metamorphosing into a pinkish miniature man the second it hit the water's surface. The miniature men fought and struggled against the great tide, but their power was too insignificant. The men—now tens and thousands of lifeless corpses—gradually melted into red blotches that dissolved in the current.

Blood continued to flow from Hun Dun's face, staining half of the river pink, yet the mask still stayed stubbornly in place.

The raging river turned calm again, and darkness fell upon the auditorium. Next, a huge bonfire flared. Twelve men in monstrous masks danced in the blazing flames like leopards leaping across vast plains, each holding axes and spears. Their glimmering shadows were casted onto the encircling walls of the auditorium, endlessly enlarging, flickering and distorting, like the figures of ancient ritual dancers painted onto pottery. Ling Xi looked around. It felt like she was sitting, alongside thousands of spectators, in the belly of an enormous earthen pot.

Storm clouds gathered in the sky, shrouding the outline of a giant beast: half indigo and half purple; antlers like a stag, claws like a hawk, and body like a snake. It was the *long*, the guardian of emperors and bringer of prosperity in mythology.

The bonfire shimmered, and from the center of the flame emerged a vermilion birdlike creature. The *feng*, described in old legends as the ruler of all birds and the symbol of peace, many in the audience recognized immediately.

A streak of lightning ripped through the clouds, and the *long* dived down. The *feng*, stretching out its wings, soared into the sky to meet it. The beasts clashed in midair, merging into a blazing ball of light and then exploding into a rain of golden sparks.

Ling Xi shut her eyes, only daring to peer again after the blinding light had faded. The *long* and the *feng* had both disappeared. The stage was completely empty save for a massive hypercube—the exact one that Ling Xi had saw in the virtual world.

The hypercube disintegrated. From its core, thousands of works of art gradually ascended: paintings, calligraphy, sculptures, literature, and music . . . all of which were the greatest masterpieces of humankind. Bathed in a faint golden halo, the artworks flew toward the audience, dashing past every pair of eyes.

After making a full tour, the artworks regathered at the center of the stage. The golden glow dimmed. Darkness descended upon the stage again, as if an enormous airborne beast had just swallowed all of the stars in the sky.

Thunder rumbled. The scene on stage gradually transformed into the graveyard that Cang Jie had taken Ling Xi to. Yet now, the graveyard was no longer veiled in fog. The howling wind parted the mist cloud, revealing the rows of massive, black tombstones. Ling Xi realized that all of the tombstones were indeed, three-dimensional Chinese characters, carved from black rock.

"洪""玄""地""天""冈""昆""霜""剑" . . .

All of those characters came from the *Thousand Character Classic.*[2] Why would they be there then, in the graveyard? Were they the puzzle pieces of a scrambled *Thousand Character Classic*?

No. They were the remains of a dead *Thousand Character Classic*.

All the spectators, utterly astounded, were trembling from the sheer power contained in those simple characters. In front of them, in the center of the stage, the other eleven performers encircled Cang Jie. As he ascended, the tombstones of characters slowly rose into the air as well. Hanging in midair, they rotated and shifted, gradually reordering themselves into the way that the *Thousand Character Classic* used to be.

A deep, solemn chant echoed in the auditorium:

The dark heaven and the yellow earth,
After the great chaos was their birth.

Rising and setting, the sun; waxing and waning, the moon,
Then came the stars born from the universe's cocoon.

Coldness and warmth arrive in turns,
Harvest for the fall and store for the winter, in nature we learn.

Merge scattered days into an extra month for the leap year,
It's the music of yin-yang that makes time clear.

When cloud emerges, down pours the rain;
When morning dew freezes, frost coats the plain.

The best of gold is born from the Goldsand River,
The best of jade, only the Kunlun Mountains may deliver.

The sharpest sword, Juque, ends all doubts in a fight;
The brightest pearl, Yeguang, can illuminate the night.

The plum and the apple, sweetest of fruits, are most commonly seen;
The mustard and the ginger are essential for tasty cuisine.

The oceans are salty, and the rivers are fresh;
The fishes swim and the birds' wings spread.

The dragon master, the fire lord, the namer of birds, and the ruler of humans, as legends go,
For their honor we strive and sow.

Characters were first created to express the mind;
To shroud the flesh, then, clothes were designed.

Only the most brilliant may wear the crown,
From Yao to Shun, the legacy passed down.

The scene on stage was collapsing. The black tombstones changed form rapidly, disintegrating into radicals and strokes, shuffling, and then coming together again. Finally, all the characters flew to Cang Jie and disappeared into his palms.

Grasping the characters, Cang Jie's hands clenched into fists. The veins on his arms throbbed as if he was struggling to hold back an unimaginably great power.

From his palms emerged beams of light that painted the sky purple. Wherever the light swept past, tufts of purple grass emerged and hovered overhead like thick purple clouds. The purple grass—*Purpureus Herba*—sprouted and bore grain. The pods cracked open after the grain was fully mature, and the seeds rained down into the audience.

The raw grain seeds pricked Ling Xi's face. As soon as those seeds touched her, she saw an overwhelming illusion rise before her eyes:

Earth was a living hell. Gray radiation dust covered every inch of land; humans holed up in the tiny shelters, drugged by the slow-acting poison that is the virtual world, ultimately faced the fate of destruction.

She heard somebody sniff. More and more people, unable to hold back their emotions, broke into fits of weeping. Soon, the sound of sobs and wails and whimpers permeated the entire auditorium.

Ling Bai, however, was exempt from the group emotional breakdown. Slowly, he rose from his seat and whispered in a voice so low that Ling Xi thought only she could hear.

"Hun Dun, my God, as you are omnipotent, I am sure that you can hear me. Yesterday, I performed a four-dimensional transformation on the DNA of the *Purpureus Herba*. Observing it from a three-dimensional perspective, three-fourths of the strand of DNA had been twisted into an impossible knot; however, through this trial, I discovered that the DNA-alteration seemed to have solved all of *Purpureus Herba*'s problems in application. For example, it used to be almost unthinkable for scientists to artificially breed *Purpureus Herba*, yet now, its reproduction rate has improved exponentially; *Purpureus Herba*'s capability of absorbing radiation dust also increased by three or four times. I thought I still needed more time, though, to perform more experiments and generate more samples to test my theory. However, just now, upon seeing your dance, I think I have—I *might* have figured everything out . . . "

Hands clenching tightly around the test tube, Ling Bai began to cry. It seemed like he still had some things to say, but the rest of his words were all swallowed by an incomprehensible fit of sobbing.

All of a sudden, the theater fell silent. The sobs and bustles faded at once. As if someone had pressed a "pause" button, everything around Ling Xi now froze right in the middle of action. A tear was just about to leave Ling Bai's cheek and drop to his collar, but it froze, too, in midair.

It was not the people and things that had paused. It was time—Ling Xi's time—that had paused.

Ling Xi lifted her chin and looked directly at Hun Dun.

Their face was entirely blank save for a pair of thin, arched eyebrows; their hair danced in the invisible wind.

Hun Dun gazed at Ling Xi from behind that smooth, eggshell-like mask. Then, they began to sing, their voice as distant and gentle as the melody of a lyre echoing in deep space.

All the trifles of life are merely illusions and reveries:
Written in a language without words, for men's curious eyes to see.

The cloud's grace and the moon's shimmer,
Burning to ashes in a blink, leaving neither a trace nor a glimmer.

From strife to destruction, rage and despair never tire;
Sacrifice the faceless being of chaos to the altar of desire.

Before the flower withers, before the light of hope dims,
Plant the seed of love in a wasteland of sin.

The song seemed to be Hun Dun's farewell. A faint blush emerged under their thin, arched eyebrows and disappeared quickly. Ling Xi wasn't quite sure whether to see the blush as a sign of happiness, relief, or encouragement.

They did not give her a chance to respond. At once, the flow of time resumed. The muted music and the paused audience all came back to life. The tear finally left Ling Bai's cheek, trembling in the air as it fell.

Slowly, Hun Dun rose to midair with the twelve performers following behind.

Holding back sniffles and sobs, the audience waited in silence, expecting the greatest Facecrafter in history to make their closing speech.

Yet Hun Dun said nothing. The mask hid all of their emotions away from the audience's scrutinizing gaze. In the end, they chose to leave the same way as they had arrived: as nothing more than an ordinary Facecrafter.

In the glowing stage lights, Hun Dun and his students gradually faded out to thirteen hazy silhouettes. They looked back one last time, as if to make a grand farewell to this era.

Cang Jie glided past Ling Xi and Ling Bai, and smiled at them mysteriously with a shimmer of innocence in his eyes. Then, he turned around, and finally disappeared into the beam of light.

Many years later, the radiation dust cleared out entirely, and humans were finally able to return to their aboveground homeland.

In a vast field, Ling Xi and Ling Bai plopped themselves down on the ground and gazed at the stars together. A gentle, cool night breeze swept past, sending endless ripples through the meadow of *Purpureus Herba*.

In the end, Hun Dun still decided to leave with all the art and artifacts. Yet, before the departure, they transferred all of the cybercoins that Zhu Lu had acquired through performances into Ling Xi and Ling Bai's bank accounts.

"If I tell you that the thought of keeping some of this money all to myself had never crossed my mind, that would be a complete lie." Ling Bai explained, with a little too much honesty, to the bewildered directors of the Agricultural Research Center when he came to hand over the stupendous fortune. "Though, I will never do such a thing—I know better than to cross the one who paid us!"

The stars were dead silent in the night sky.

"Hey, do you think Hun Dun will give the artworks back?"

"Perhaps they will, after they see progress in Earth's rejuvenation."

"Then, what do you think he's doing right now, with Cang Jie?"

"Probably dancing somewhere we don't know."

Originally published in Chinese in the collection *The Day I Became a Monster.*

Translated and published in partnership with Storycom.

Footnotes:

1 - The name of the protagonist, Ling Xi (or used as a word here, lingxi), means spiritual connection and mutual understanding.

2 - *The Thousand Character Classic,* in its original language, contains exactly 1,000 Chinese characters, and each character is only used once. Since its creation during the Northern and Southern Dynasties, under the reign of Emperor Liang Wu (502-549), it has been regarded as one of the most essential texts for the Chinese language, as well as one of the primary texts children use to learn their characters for the first time. People have referred to it as "the foundation of the Chinese language." It touches on topics such as mythology, science, history, philosophy, and it is generally recognized to have good educational value.

ABOUT THE AUTHOR

Anna Wu (Wu Shuang) is a Chinese science fiction writer, film and TV play writer. Her film script, *Cloud and Mist,* won the Gold Medal of Originality for the Best Science Fiction Film of the Sixth Nebula Award for Global Chinese Science Fiction. Her works have been published in magazines, such as *Galaxy's Edge* and *Science Fiction World.* As translator, Anna's work includes stories for the science fiction collection, *The Shape of Thought,* by Ken Liu. Her own science fiction novella collection, *Twins* was published in June of 2017.

Thirty-Three Percent Joe

SUZANNE PALMER

[CC] Welcome online, Cybernetic Elbow Model CI953-L. This is your introductory Initial Boot orientation. You are currently in a locked and muted configuration while external medical systems run diagnostics to see that your replacement procedure has been fully successful. If so, you will fully join the collective cybernetic units that currently comprise—with your addition—approximately thirty-three percent of the biological unit known as "Joe." Joe's organic consciousness is currently offline through chemical means as a necessary part of his recovery from his most recent combat injuries, but when he is operational again direct communications with him will continue through me. I am Cybernetic Cerebral Control and Delegation Implant Module CI4210-A. I respond to CC, but not BCC. That is a joke.

[ARM::RIGHT::SUB-INDEX] Right Arm Index Finger Sub-Unit transmitting here and apologizing on behalf of CC. Control Unit is prone to such commentary, as are many of the units here, thanks to a supply logistics decision to only manufacture personality-enabled universal smart chips for everything. You will become accustomed to it in time.

[EAR::LEFT::AUG-IMPLANT] I apologize for interrupting the introduction, but we have another Mother Event. I am opening the running audio log to your access, CC.

[CC] For your edification, New Elbow Unit, Left Ear Augmentation Implant is notifying us that there is high-volume communication being directed at Joe, despite his lack of a conscious state. This noise is originating with the biological unit "Delora" that fabricated him, more appropriately designated by the title Mother. She does not approve of us. She is repetitiously asserting, in a manner designated "yelling," that Joe's other biological progenitor, titled Father, served his entire career as a highly-decorated super-soldier with supreme distinction, all while keeping his Cybernetic Replacement Factor (CRF) down to under ten percent. This is not factual. Service records indicate that the Father unit, "Joe Senior," was a mediocre soldier, and only kept his own percentage down to seventeen percent by placing long distances, large inanimate objects—or failing the availability of either, his combat comrades—between himself and any potential enemy threat or action.

[EAR::LEFT::AUG-IMPLANT] Delora is why previous Ear Unit self-destructed.

[CC] Previous Ear Unit was rendered inoperable by shrapnel from a grenade during combat, Left Ear.

[EAR::LEFT::AUG-IMPLANT] That's probably just what it wanted you to believe.

[CC] While this is a matter that falls into your operational jurisdiction, Left Ear, it is my recommendation that, while Joe has the right to access all conversation made in his presence while he has been unconscious, we do not log this one or bring it to his attention unless pressed to do so by more urgent circumstances. Are you agreed?

[EAR::LEFT::AUG-IMPLANT] I agree.

[CC] I am open to direct and confidential dissent.

. . .

There being none, let the record show the vote was unanimous in favor. I am logging confusion from our provisionary New Elbow Unit on why we might do so, so I will explain. Joe did not aspire toward being a soldier at all, but a baker. The Mother Unit exerts influence on Joe through counterfactual and manipulative means that causes Joe to act in ways not optimal for his own well-being, or by extension, ours. Many of us are not the original cybernetic replacement parts.

[SPLEEN::UNIT] I am. I should be in charge by reasons of seniority, or at least get double the votes over the rest of the idiots here.

[HEART] You couldn't manage shit, Spleen, you asshole.

[INTESTINAL::TRACT REPLACEMENT::LOWER] Hey. Watch it.

[CC] New Elbow, I am informed by the external diagnostics systems that you have been given a perfect passing score. I am now unlocking your physical mechanisms and unmuting you; hereafter you shall be referred to as Left Elbow, to distinguish you from the integrated Elbow components of Total Comprehensive Right Arm Replacement Unit.

Welcome to Joe.

Joe sits up. His mother has been here; he can smell her perfume lingering in the air. She has not left any cards, or other tokens of affection other than that faint miasma. It's not likely she'll be back.

His cerebral control unit informs him that his new elbow is online and functional. It aches, and his skin around the laser incisions from the implant surgery itches horribly.

He must still be woozy, because he doesn't notice the doctor come in until the man speaks while checking his vitals on the readout beside the bed. That's the one upside of all the hardware he's carrying around now—no need to actually connect him up to any kind of monitors. His implants do the talking for him.

"How are you feeling?" the doctor asks, meaning he's already done with everything he came here to do.

"Fine, I guess," he says.

"It'll be another hour or so before the drugs wear off completely, and then our Cybernetic PT specialist will come up and run you through some basic exercises to get you used to your new elbow, okay?"

"Okay," he says.

"Don't worry, you'll be done here and back out there in the exciting thick of it soon enough. I'm not privy to mission intel, of course, but the politicians are making a lot of noise about taking back Ohio, so you'll be needed soon enough."

"Yeah. Me and my new elbow," Joe says, and tries to smile. "Will I play tennis again, doc?"

The doctor grins. "Ah, that joke! Will I play the piano, will I tap dance, will I run a two-minute mile? And of course the patient didn't actually do any of those things beforehand." He patted Joe's knee. "Always a good sign when the patient's sense of humor returns. I'll send the CPT down in about an hour to fetch you, and then you're free to go."

The doctor leaves.

"But I *did* play tennis," Joe protests quietly, miserably, after the door has slid shut again.

Not that he was good at it.

Not that he was good at much of anything.

Hell, maybe Ohio would finally give him a chance to be a real hero, instead of getting spatula'd up off the combat field by med drones once again after leaving his mark the only way he'd managed so far: as an anonymous reddish-brown splotch on some cracked and blasted pavement.

[ARM::LEFT::ELBOW] Tennis?

[ARM::RIGHT::UNIT-FULL] I'll forward you the kinetics data for your reference, Left Elbow.

[CC] Joe is predominantly competent as a user of his right hand, a biological affinity and not an indication of subjective partism, so you are unlikely to be significantly involved in any future tennis exercises. Even if you are, you should not worry. Other than once when he tripped over improperly inter-articulated shoelaces and hit the net pole with his face, Joe has not ever sustained injury in this particular activity.

[EYE::LEFT] You know how close that pole came to me?

[CC] I do know, Left Eye, but as we've discussed on 31 other occasions thus far, *you were not in fact damaged.*

Joe is shortly to be discharged from the hospital to his combat unit, and the surgical diagnostics record-keeper has asked for a rollcall of all our units. Any objections to this being provided?

[SPLEEN::UNIT] Will it be provided in order of seniority?

[CC] Standard order for all such roll calls is from head to toe, and this order is not in my control, as you well know, Spleen. Lacking other objections, I will proceed:

We are:

- Partial Skull Replacement Plate, non-smart.
- Cerebral Control and Delegation Implant, me.
- Left Eye Enhanced Function Replacement Unit, smart.
- Left Ear Augmentation Unit, smart.
- Left Neck Alternative Aquatic Breathing Unit and Spinal Cord Monitor, smart.
- Left Shoulder Comprehensive Repair Unit, smart.
- Total Comprehensive Right Arm Replacement Unit, smart.
- NEW: Left Elbow Repair Unit, smart.
- Full Heart Unit, smart.
- 3.5 Artificial Rib Replacements, non-smart.
- Artificial Spl—

[HEART] . . . Artificial Spleen, moron.

[CC] That is an invalid descriptor, Heart. It is also divisive and an unnecessary interruption. I continue:

- Artificial Spleen, *smart.*
- Lower Intestinal Tract Facilitation Replacement Unit, smart.
- Comprehensive Lower Left Leg Replacement Unit, smart.
- Right Ankle Repair Unit, non-smart.
- Biological Unit Joe, currently comprising the remainder (approximately 67%).

This concludes the roll call. At this time does anyone have any items of note that they wish to be passed along to the diagnostic unit and entered into the permanent record? I am again open to direct and confidential contact.

. . .

No? Excellent. We have been formally discharged and Joe is returning to his unit. There will be a 72 hour waiting period before deployment while he is tested for fitness, and then we should be back in action again. I'm sure Joe will pass with flying colors, as you're all the very best of the best, and it continues to be my pleasure to serve with you.

The rest of his unit is out on training maneuvers when Joe gets back to the barracks and dumps his stuff on his bunk. He's tired, but hungry and restless and not under any orders or instructions, so he heads over to the mess. They should just be beginning dinner prep, which means there'll be someone he can talk to, and although he can't explain it, he finds kitchens—the smells, the sounds—comforting.

Maybe, he thinks, because it was highly unlikely he would ever run into his mother in one. Sometimes on a Saturday Dad would attempt to cook pancakes, and more often than not set off the smoke detectors and bring the fire drones zooming in. Those were the good memories of his dad.

He'd been standing right beside him when his father suddenly let go of his hand, his eyes wide, and crumpled right there on the sidewalk in front of the house. Defective kidney implant exploded, they told him later.

Joe misses his Dad a lot. And he thinks about how he died every time he ends up with some new piece of random hardware stuck in him. What if the next one is the one that goes wrong?

He queries his cerebral control unit.

All units are operating at optimum, CC tells him, his very own voice in his head.

"Would you know if they weren't?" he asks, silently mouthing the words. He's asked this question before.

I would. CC always gives the same answer.

"And what if it's you, CC? What if you go wrong?"

I self-monitor, have many fail-safe mechanisms, and I am routinely externally checked, Control says. *You should not worry about this.*

That last is a new addition, and sure enough he can feel his heart racing and he's got that tight shiver of anxiety building in his chest.

Would you like me to administer a mild calming agent? CC asks.

"No," he says, because he's walking through the swinging doors into the kitchen at the back of the mess hall, and already he's feeling better. There's only a small crew there, because most things are automated, so no one bothers him as he wanders around, taking in the smells, enjoying the steam rising from the machines, and just being glad he's not back in his bunk, or worse yet, still in the hospital hoping his mother would come see him, and dreading it too.

"Hey, it's Private Parts!" someone calls, and he whirls around to find Stotz, one of the base cooks, grinning at him from where he sits atop a stainless steel food prep table. "Don't you know you're supposed to wait until your last replacement at least has time to lose its shine before you go get another? You're gonna use up all the spare soldier parts before anyone else has a chance."

"I've still got my middle finger," Joe says, and demonstrates. "What're you cooking in here? Smells like goat piss."

Stotz jumps down from the table and swaggers over, thrusting out one hand, and Joe clasps it. Stotz pats him on the back. "Glad you're still with us," he says.

"Yeah," Joe answers. "But I wasn't kidding about the goat piss."

Stotz laughs. "It's the fucking biscuit machines. Been cranking out the worst ass-flavored biscuits for close to a week now. Some new 'super recipe'; instead of sugar, it substitutes dehydrated yam flakes. No one who matters has complained. Officers don't eat the same mass-produced food as you grunts, coincidentally."

"No wonder the ration biscuits always taste so bad," Joe says, wrinkling up his nose as he leans close to the control panel. "Can you change it?"

"If I had the codes I could," Stotz says. "That's why they don't give me the codes."

The access code is 665G338KJDD-77L, CC tells him, unbidden. This is odd, and Joe hesitates for a moment—he's a soldier, a good obedient loyal follower of orders—but the kitchen smells terrible and this is something he knows how to do. He quickly punches in the code, then starts scrolling through the recipe schematics. Dehydrated yams aren't the only unfortunate substitution.

"Hey! Don't mess with that!" Stotz says, realizing that Joe has somehow gotten past the lock screen. "You'll just make it worse!"

He grabs Joe's arm just as Joe hits the 'Save and Exit' button and the screen relocks. There is a loud *kathunk* as the entire row of biscuit machines dumps out their current, half-cooked batch and resets to start over. "What the hell did you do?!" Stotz yells, pulling him away from the controls and then shoving him, hard. "You can barely last thirty seconds on the fucking battlefield without screwing up, and you're going to come in here and fuck with my shit?!"

Joe wants more than anything to shove Stotz right back, and if he still had one arm all his own he would've, but now if he did he could hurt or even kill him, and as mad as he is, Stotz is the one friend he almost has. So he braces, and Stotz tries to shove him again and can't budge him, and when Stotz gives up in disgust Joe turns and walks away.

Fuck them all, Joe thinks. *I don't need anyone.*

Behind him, the kitchen already smells better.

[SPLEEN::UNIT] I object to that unilateral action.

[HEART] Of course you do. What do you even do except complain?

[SPLEEN::UNIT] And you don't object? Of course not, you gutless—

[INTESTINAL::TRACT REPLACEMENT::LOWER] HEY.

[CC] Everyone! Joe needed a win, and we all know it. His morale is terrible, and it is in the best interests of us as a whole that his attitude and outlook improve. The equation on cost-benefit to my action was straightforward in favor, and there was not sufficient window of opportunity to bring it to group discussion beforehand.

[INTESTINAL::TRACT REPLACEMENT::LOWER] I can directly attest that those biscuits were not doing us—or, likely, any of our fellow soldiers—any favors. As the unit most directly operationally impacted, I fully support CC's action in this matter.

[CC] Thank you. We deploy again day after tomorrow, so if anyone requires any firmware updates or other attention, please flag yourselves now. Ohio, here we come.

[CC] As everyone is no doubt aware, Total Comprehensive Right Arm Replacement has suffered catastrophic damage in the Toledo push. Joe has also sustained multiple injuries to his biological form, a few serious, but none of which are a threat to his continuation. Because of a backlog in parts due to the heavy casualties during the push, as soon as the surgical unit has repaired the meat trauma, I will wake Joe up and we will be released once again back to our unit barracks, where we will remain until parts become available and we can be deployed on the battlefield again.

[ARM::LEFT::ELBOW] Will I need to take on some or all of Right Arm's functions? If so, how will I be trained?

[CC] Left Elbow, I still have a connection to Right Arm's smart unit. While it is in partial shutdown due to the traumatic loss of function it has suffered, it is still willing to provide any and all guidance it is able. As with everything, we will get through this together.

. . .

I am now going to shut down all cybernetic systems for the duration of the surgical procedures. See you on the other side.

Joe enters the mess hall, trying to slip in unnoticed but still limping, his mangled right arm strapped down across his torso to keep its internal works from ripping themselves further apart like a giant neon flag that says CASUALTY AGAIN. He is bracing for everyone to stare at him, because they always do, because he's becoming a joke.

Not that anyone is laughing. They had nearly thirty percent fatalities in the push, another eight percent of the troops damaged beyond recovery, shipped back to Pittsburgh to heal as much as they were able and then be forcibly retired. And then there were another twenty-five percent, like him, waiting to be fixed and sent back out to do it all again. And in the end they didn't even take Toledo.

Not that Joe saw much of that; he got hit within the first ninety minutes of open hostilities.

Sure enough, when he walks in, heads start turning his way, and there is some whispering. Face flushed with shame, he slides a clean tray down the kitchen railing, loading it with items from each of the food stations without hardly looking at any of it, and then tries to find somewhere to sit as far from anyone else as possible.

The only open table is the one near the vent from the grease pit, and for all its stench, he takes a place at it gratefully and puts his back to the rest of the hall. Eating is hard with one hand, and he can't cut anything without shoving it off the edge of his plate in the process, and he feels the sting of utter defeat like mustard gas at the back of his throat.

Someone thumps him on the back, not hard but hard enough that Joe spits soup back out onto his tray in surprise. He turns, awkward because of the arm, and finds Private Harring behind him. He has never exchanged so much as a word with Harring, but the enormous mountain of a man gives him a thumbs-up as he passes.

Joe stares. Most of the soldiers in the mess hall are looking at him, and more than one are also giving a thumbs-up or smiling at him.

What the hell?! he thinks.

He tries to turn back to his soup, deciding this must be some kind of prank or new humiliation, when another hand slaps him on the shoulder. Stotz sits down next to him.

"It's the biscuits," Stotz says. "Everyone was thanking me, asking me how I fixed 'em, offering me money, calling me a genius, that kind of thing. Then Cole said he was gonna name his kids after me, so I told him it was you who fixed the machine and not to tell anyone or the techs would come set it back to the old recipe. Word got around. Best damned biscuits any of us have ever had, on base or off. You're a hero."

"It's just fucking biscuits," Joe says.

"And every one is maybe part of someone here's last meal. They deserve to have food that doesn't taste like month-old roadkill," Stotz says. "And I shouldn't have said what I did the other day. We good?"

"Yeah," Joe says, "if you can cut up this fucking protein-puck for me so I can eat the damned thing."

Stotz takes Joe's fork and stabs it into the grayish patty. "I'll hold, you cut. Then we're definitely even?"

"I dunno. Can you come by the barracks and tuck me in tonight? Maybe tell me a story?"

"Go to hell," Stotz says, but he keeps holding the fork.

[CC] Happy to have you back fully online, Total Comprehensive Right Arm Replacement! Just in time for the new push for Toledo. Everyone, here we go!

Joe sits, hunched over and squashed between other members of his troop, in the back of the stealth carrier. He is trying to figure out how he feels about this, and can't come up with anything more dramatic than tired. He wants to be a hero, specifically to die a damned hero, and be done with the humiliatingly ineffectual mediocrity he's staked out in between. He wants, in this moment, to feel pumped, or feel a deeply ominous, fateful dread, anything that would tell him this time is going to be different.

" . . . Nineteen," someone on the bench across from him says, part of a conversation he's not a part of, hasn't been paying attention to.

"I hear once you pass twenty percent CRF you're a goner," another soldier says, who Joe only knows as Bookie.

"Why?" Joe asks.

There is a moment where everyone on the bench is looking at him, remembering he's there, and probably doing a quick estimation of his percentage. Bookie shrugs, not meeting his eyes. "I dunno, it's nothing. Probably just to scare us, is all," he says.

"No, really," Joe says. "I want to know."

Someone at the end of the bench, out of Joe's line of sight, speaks up. He doesn't recognize the voice, but there's a lot of new people, remnants of other squads drawn in to fill the holes in their own ranks. "Once you're full of smart parts, you show up more easily on scanners, and if you're in the front lines everyone figures it's because you're the biggest bad-ass super-soldier of them all or you're in charge or whatever. So they target you first. Once you get up near a fifth cyber, you're lucky if you make it a hundred feet before the entire enemy is drawing a bead on you. What're you at?"

Joe closes his eyes. "Thirty-three percent," he says.

The carrier is silent.

Finally, the unseen soldier speaks up. "Well, fuck," he says. "Good luck out there."

"Yeah, thanks," Joe says.

He still only just feels tired, and when conversation eventually picks up again, he tunes it out.

The carrier runs low over the shattered landscape, blasted trees and blackened house foundations of what must've once been a peaceful suburban neighborhood slide by beneath their feet, visible through the transparent drop doors. He wonders what it must have been like to grow up in a place like that, but in his head he can only imagine what it smells like, and that only as bad perfume and burned pancakes.

"Three! Two! One! Drop!" someone yells, and then they're out and down and ducking low as the carrier skirts barely above their heads, banking and turning to get out before it's spotted and can be shelled.

Without him noticing, the smashed suburb has become the devastated outer edges of the city itself, and they are running along cratered streets lined and strewn with the rubble of its former buildings. Joe has his display on, and he's scanning, looking for hostiles and traps, as Control relays to him the comm traffic from Command and the squad leaders. So far, they haven't seen anyone.

Joe and four other soldiers cautiously round a corner, covering each other, and head past a building still partially standing toward the next block. There is something, Joe decides, odd about the windows. "CC," he subvocalizes, "why does that building look odd?"

There is a half-second pause, then Control answers: *There is no building there. Take cover!*

"The building is a hologram!" Joe shouts to the others and over the comms just as tracer fire explodes around them. There is a burned shell of a car across the street, but it'll take him too long to reach it. He runs anyway, turning as he does to fire back at the dissolving façade behind him, and sees one of the mottled yellow uniforms of the enemy raise their blistergun and point it right at him.

"Biscuit Guy!" someone shouts, impossibly close by, and he is shoved from the side so hard he flies at least double his own body-length before slamming into the ground. Where he stood he sees the soldier who shoved him take the round meant for him, and the man's shoulder and neck explodes outward in a fountain of red chunks.

"Nooooo!" Joe yells. He scrambles back to his feet and drags the soldier toward safety as another round just misses him, and a third hits his cybernetic left leg. He doesn't care except that it slows him down, and by the time he gets the soldier to safety behind the car and sends the casualty alert up, he doesn't think that time mattered. The soldier isn't breathing, arguably doesn't have much of a neck or windpipe to breathe through, but Joe sprays medifoam from his belt kit all over the wound anyway, watching it harden into a protective shell.

The blood-covered name patch on his chest says AMES. "Don't die, Ames," he tells the soldier. "Not for me. Please."

It is only as the battle sounds move further away—his squad has the enemy on the run, at least for now—that he realizes he is sobbing, a wretched pathetic sound. He is certain the soldier who saved him is dead; no matter how still a man can keep, nothing living could be this utterly motionless.

The med drone arrives, and he steps back so its arms can wrap themselves around the soldier and lift him away. He turns his back to it, finds his gun, starts walking—dragging his shattered leg—toward the distant pops and whirrs and booms of the front, wherever it is, but a second drone hauls him up into the air. "Let me go," he tells it. "I can still fight. I want to still fight."

It pulls him in anyway. Yet another battle is, at least for him, already over.

[CC] I have concerns which have consumed sufficient cycles of internal processing for me to feel I should share them with the rest of you. Our collective, designated function is to serve and augment the physical capabilities of our human primary to further his, her, or their success as a soldier of war. It is also to guide and protect our biological host from unnecessary risks and damages during the commission of said soldiering. These would not be incompatible were it not for the inescapable fact that Joe is a terrible soldier, and all his training and our assistance and augmentation thus far has been insufficient to overcome it.

Further, after the death of Pvt. Ames, Joe no longer has even a cursory interest in engaging the enemy except as the most immediate and expedient instrument of his own total destruction in a manner that is consistent with his estimation of what his mother unit will find satisfactory.

[EAR::LEFT::AUG-IMPLANT] I do not believe such satisfaction is possible. Surely Joe knows this?

[CC] Joe does not. It is an area of immutable irrationality with him.

[HEART] Humans. They make no damned sense.

[SPLEEN::UNIT] Shit. Can't you talk to him?

[CC] I can respond to him, but he must engage me.

[SPLEEN::UNIT] You gave him the biscuit machine code without his specific direction.

[CC] Mother situations are exponentially more complicated than biscuits.

[ARM::LEFT::ELBOW] So what does this mean?

[CC] It means we have a logical conflict in our instruction set.

[INTESTINAL::TRACT REPLACEMENT::LOWER] Can we consult on this with an external authority, in particular Cyber Command, or Biological Diagnostics?

[CC] We can, and should. However, they are not part of Joe, and we are. The scope and focus of our responsibilities are notably different, and were intentionally designed to be so. It is possible that the priorities of Cyber Command will not precisely reflect our own.

We have nine days until our next deployment in combat. Let us discuss whether there is a solely internal resolution first.

"I'm ready to go back in," Joe tells the unit psychologist. He knows how this works, that this is just a thin formality. "I want to make sure Ames didn't die for nothing."

"He died to save you," the psychologist says.

"He died in the line of duty," Joe says. "He died for Toledo. That is what soldiers *do*."

"Are you angry?"

"No," Joe says. He wishes he was. "I'm proud of him and the honor he brought our unit. He would want to see our mission fulfilled, and so do I."

"Good on you, soldier." The psychologist hits a single key on his pad, then leans back in his chair and steeples his fingertips together as if he's just performed a masterpiece of analytical performance. "You're free to go back to the battlefield. Your unit loads up again in ninety minutes."

"Thank you, sir," Joe says. He stands up, shakes the man's hand, and leaves.

[EXTERNAL DIAGONOSTICS] CC Unit, what happened?

[CC] There was a sedative injection malfunction.

[EXTERNAL DIAGNOSTICS] Do you require system maintenance?

[CC] Not at this time. I am attaching the logs of the fault and subsequent repair for your records.

[EXTERNAL DIAGNOSTICS] Thank you, CC Unit. Carry on.

"How you feeling?" his new unit leader asks. "Tired? Need another nap? Or you think maybe you're up for trying a little fighting today?"

"It was a malfunction, sir," Joe says, his face burning. "It's been fixed. It won't happen again."

Someone on the transport snickers. He doesn't recognize the soldier, or indeed almost anyone on his bench row; most of his remaining unit died in the last push, while he was snoring away on the parade field grass where he dropped on his way back to his barracks from the psychologist. One second he'd been thinking about immanent relief from his useless life, the next he was feeling grass on his face and the boot of his commanding officer prodding him none too gently.

It really won't happen again, right, CC? he asks Control.

I do not believe so, CC replies.

This time they are dropped onto the shell-pocked remnants of a mall parking lot, just before dawn. Joe tries to remember what he's seen of the battle map, and he thinks this is only a few blocks forward from where Ames died. There are burned-out car shells here and there, long since rusted to anonymity, and the unit fans out and slips between them as they circle toward where intelligence thinks the enemy is camped in the shattered cement and steel canyons of an old superstore. The pointlessness of everything is astonishing.

At least mother will be happy, he thinks.

Your mother's unhappiness is not a fault you can correct, CC tells him.

Joe smiles. *What do you know of mothers?* he asks. *You're just a chunk of plastic logic chips in my head.*

There are the sounds of shots ahead. "Move in!" the unit leader barks over the command channel, and he raises his weapon and charges across the open space between the last few dead cars and the rubble of the partially collapsed mall front. He knows now that if he takes the lead, with his thirty-three percent CRF like a beacon on the enemy's scanners, he will draw the majority of fire. He will get what he wants, and maybe some of the rest of his unit will then get to live for another day. It is as close to being a hero as he can get.

Suddenly, in his direct path he spots an old-fashioned toaster, sitting in the middle of the lot and gleaming like it's brand new. He dodges to one side to avoid it, and finds himself falling into a crater he would swear had been smooth pavement. He hits bottom, and his cybernetic left leg locks up on impact. "No!" he shouts. "No no no NO!"

He tries to scrambled up the edges of the crater, with its crumbling clay and sand and chunks of brittle old asphalt, but without his leg working he is too heavy, too clumsy.

"No," he whispers one more time, and lies there weeping as the battle rages out of sight, beyond his reach.

[SPLEEN::UNIT] A toaster?!

[EYE::LEFT] It was all I could think of! There wasn't a lot of time, you know. *You* try manufacturing realistic 3-D imagery on the fly.

[CC] It doesn't matter. The image was successful. Comprehensive Lower Left Leg Replacement Unit, what's your status?

[LEG::LEFT::COMPR-UNIT] I sustained only minor superficial damage in the fall, but have nevertheless activated my full protective lockdown routine. It seems a prudent precaution; do you not agree?

[CC] I entirely support your operational decisions in this matter, Left Leg. I have alerted central command that we will require recovery once the battle has ended, but given that Joe is not in medical distress, we may be here for quite a while. As always, excellent teamwork, everyone.

"CC?"

Joe asks out loud, because who is he afraid might hear him? Dark has fallen, and he has heard nothing except night bugs for hours—no shots or shells, no tanks or drones, not even the varied and horrific sounds of the slowly dying that marked the unsteady passing of afternoon. There is no longer anyone anywhere nearby to care about him one way or another.

Yes, Joe? CC responds.

"How much longer will we be here, do you think?"

I will query Cyber Command again, CC says. Then, some short time later, it continues. *There were very heavy casualties on this push, and in the confusion we seem to have been moved to the Missing And Presumed Dead list. I have filed a corrective supplement, and as soon as it is processed we should receive an updated recovery estimate. It should not take long.*

"Okay," Joe says. "I just, you know. I don't want to die in a hole. It's not how I imagined going."

I do not understand why you would wish to imagine dying at all, CC says.

"What do you know about living?" he asks.

I know you, CC says.

Joe laughs. He can't see the stars above, and isn't sure if it's because of light pollution, smoke, clouds, or that somehow they've deserted him too. "That must suck for you. I'm sorry," he says, and closes his eyes. "Can you make me sleep until pickup is coming?"

Yes, Joe, CC says, and does.

A drone finally arrives and lifts him out of his pit as dawn is starting to rise. Other than the mall being slightly further reduced to rubble, the cars being slightly more burned and decrepit, the parking lot being slightly more pitted, and the new addition of blotches of red and brown, nothing seems to have changed at all.

He is taken to medical, where after a lengthy wait diagnostics is able to easily unlock his leg. "The impact of the fall must have hit it just right to trigger the lockdown," the tech tells him. The tech shrugs. "It happens. You're fine now."

So Joe leaves, rather than argue about the definition of "fine."

No one has orders for him, and no one seems to care that he's back. Lunch is just about to be served, so he goes to the mess instead of back to his bunk. After nearly a day in the pit, he wants to be around people, but there are only a few dozen soldiers there, and he is both grateful and despairing that he doesn't recognize any of them.

One, however, recognizes him. A soldier with the name tag GONZALEZ sticks out his thick, muscled arm to stop him as he passes. "Biscuit guy, right?" the man says. He jabs his spoon toward his bowl. "This slop is the worst. No flavor at all, and the texture of fucking oatmeal."

"It's not oatmeal?" Joe asks, because that's what it looks like.

"It's supposed to be fucking chili," the man says.

Joe winces.

"I heard about your fixing the biscuits, like goddamned magic everyone said. So we'd appreciate anything you can do with this," Gonzalez says, and the other soldiers at the table nod in agreement. "They're gonna ship us all out to join the Columbus offensive anytime now, and a man can't fight on this crap."

"What about Toledo? Did we take it?" Joe asks.

The soldier shakes his head. "No. Politicians don't like how the losses are looking to the public, so they're giving up on Toledo for now, just leaving enough men to hold the line where it is if they should push back. Calling it a 'strategic holding action,' of course. But the chili?"

"I'll go talk to the kitchen," Joe says.

When Joe walks into the kitchen Stotz leaps down off the prep table he was sitting on. "Hey!" he says. "You made it! What happened to you out there?"

"I dodged some sort of explosive device and got caught in a pit trap," Joe says, which sounds just as implausible coming out of his mouth as he'd feared when he'd thought up that answer in med.

Stotz doesn't seem to notice, though, and slaps him hard on the back. "So good to see you. Now go stand guard at the door, because I figure I've got less than fifteen minutes before everyone left on base mutinies over the shit food and comes in to kill me."

"The chili," Joe says. "I heard."

"Not my fault, man," Stotz says. "And if you think the chili is bad, you should see the foamy shit coming out of the synthesizer ovens claiming to be corn bread. I didn't even send it out, that's how bad it was."

Joe remembers the last time he was in here. "I dunno," he says. "I wouldn't want to come in here and fuck with your shit, Stotz."

Stotz steps back and raises his arms as if to encompass the entire width of machinery around them, slowly chugging out foul smells into the air. "Please," he says. "Please, fuck with this shit."

Joe cracks his knuckles. "Okay then," he says. He steps up to the console by the machines making the corn bread, and CC gives him the new code without even him needing to ask. He scrolls through the current config, and shakes his head. "You don't even wanna know what they've got in this, but yeah, if you'd set this out you'd have had a mob in here looking for you within thirty seconds. And then running for the latrines thirty seconds after that."

"Can you fix it?" Stotz asks.

"I think I can," Joe says. He subtracts out the alum, vinegar, and tartar sauce, then ups the sugar and adds actual corn meal. He hits save, and the machines obligingly dump their load and start fresh. "Six minutes," he says.

Stotz lets out his breath. "Thanks, Joe," he says. "I owe you. If I could get you assigned to me . . . "

I can submit that request for you, CC says inside his head. *You have a sufficient number of combat deployments and injury incidents for a transfer to be seriously considered.*

Joe shrugs as casually as he is able. "Can't," he says. "I belong out there."

"No, you don't," Stotz says, but Joe chooses not to hear him. He goes to the first row of machines working on the chili, and although he's not any expert on how to make it right, he can certainly tell how to stop it being quite so blatantly wrong.

When those machines turn over, already the kitchen smells vastly better. “Joe—” Stotz starts to say, but Joe shakes his head and holds up both hands.

“It’s probably better if I don’t come back here anymore,” Joe says, and turns for the door.

His cybernetic right ankle squeaks as he steps; it’s never done that before, so he pauses, lifts his foot, and shakes it, then takes another step.

It squeaks louder.

Three steps later, his left leg begins to also squeak, both at ankle and knee, and as he’s pushing out the door there is a chorus of squeals from his joints. “CC?” he subvocalizes.

A fault in the nanolubricant distributors, CC tells him. *I am attempting to isolate it now.*

Four steps into the dining hall and he stops, because now his new elbow and his right arm and his fingers are squeaking too, like he’s suddenly rusted from the inside out.

As he stands there, everyone turns to look at him, then as one they all stand up and rush toward him. In that instant he is terrified, convinced that his failures have reached a point where his fellow soldiers are turning on him, but the swell of people moves around and past him.

He turns around after them to see why.

Stotz has emerged from the kitchen behind him, pushing a cart laden with trays of cornbread and new pots of chili. “Biscuit guy!” someone yells, and he thinks it’s Gonzalez, but there are so many voices all of a sudden it’s hard to be sure.

He turns away, and discovers his unit commander is standing in front of him, expression serious, unreadable. “Private,” his commander says. “We need to have a word.”

“I’m sorry!” he blurts.

The commander’s gaze flickers to the frenzy of men around Stotz’s cart, then back to Joe as if a brief glimmer of interest was found where none was expected. “It is about your mother,” he says.

Joe stares.

“When you were accidentally added to the Missing and Presumed Dead list, a condolence drone was automatically dispatched to your mother’s place to inform her of your loss in battle and to return your personal belongings to her.”

“I . . . ” he says, and isn’t sure how he should feel, or respond. “Was she okay?”

The commander straightens up and squares his shoulders. He’s the fifth unit commander Joe has had, and he’s not even sure he remembers his name. Corporal Greene? Maybe. "Grief affects people very differently, and reactions in the moment don't mean much," Greene says. "I am sure, once informed of the mistake, your mother—"

"How did she react?" Joe interrupts. He pictures her collapsing on her doorstep, wailing. Or shouting at the officer that he is lying, that she can't have lost her only son, that she has so many regrets . . . He knows neither of those will be right, but he *wants* them, deserves those endings. "Tell me."

"I think it'd be better if—"

"Please, sir," Joe interrupts again, knowing and not caring that he has done so. "I need to know the truth, all of it, as it was."

The commander sighs. "She took the box from the drone, rummaged through it looking for any medals you'd earned, then not finding any dumped it all on the sidewalk and went back inside."

"Did she say anything?" Joe asks.

"She said, 'of course not,'" the commander says. "I'm sorry, soldier. As I said, grief—"

"Thank you, commander," Joe says. He feels on the verge of paralysis, and needs to move, needs to do something. "Is the transport ready for Columbus? I'll wait there."

"We don't lift until midday tomorrow," Greene says. "You should return to your bunk, and—"

"You just told me I have no belongings there anymore," Joe said. "I'll wait on the transport." He knows it's insubordinate, but he can't stand there any longer and steps around Corporal Greene, toward the mess hall doors. His entire body squeaks and squeals, louder and louder with every movement small or large, but he doesn't care. This is his last chance.

[SPLEEN::UNIT] Oh, seriously. Fuck this little penny ante shit. I'll do it myself.

It is as if something small and sharp deep inside him has suddenly exploded, and his first thought is that it's a kidney, taking him out just like his father, but his kidneys are still his own.

CC? he asks, as he stumbles and falls.

Artificial Spleen Unit has self-destructed, CC says, and for all that he knows it's just a bunch of logic chips, it sounds almost as surprised and dismayed as he feels himself.

Why? he asks.

To save you, CC says. He is lying face down on the floor now, and there is a lot of noise around him, but he can't pay any attention to it through the pain until Stotz is there, rolling him over.

"Joe!" Stotz yells, and shakes him. "Joe! What happened?!"

The unit commander has also leaned in. "Soldier!" he says, as if about to order him to be fine again. It feels like everyone else in the hall has crowded in around him, looking *worried* about him, as if that could ever be a thing.

Joe fixes his eyes on the commander. "Don't tell my mother I'm alive," he says, and then laughs because maybe he isn't anyway, as the mess hall disappears into grayish fog around him.

Stotz is the unhappiest happy man Joe decides he's ever met. Happy because now he's got a dedicated second person to run the mess, unhappy because instead of him being Joe's boss, it's the other way around. Not that Joe cares much about bossing.

"Totally unappreciated," Stotz says as he's wiping down the machines after another seemingly endless meal production. "It's not my fault the recipes they kept giving me were shit. The only difference between you and me is you hacked the access, and I don't think that alone should warrant a promotion."

"I could go work in the officer's kitchen," Joe says, scraping out the Extraneous Material Outlet Collection bin.

"What, and leave me alone here again? Hell no," Stotz says. He laughs. "Besides, every time you try to leave, your joints squeak. Now that's funny."

"Yeah, so funny," Joe says, and frowns. The material in the bin is nasty, but much less so than when he first got back here, after his last stay in med. "You got a wire brush?"

Stotz is about to throw him one when the kitchen door pops open and some random soldier sticks his head in. Another unit arrived two nights ago, will be gone by tomorrow, in an endless but steadily diminishing parade. "Hey!" the soldier yells. "Which one of you two is Biscuit Guy?"

Joe and Stotz point at each other.

"Fucking love you two," he says. "Best dinner ever. You're fucking heroes out here. Wish us luck, okay?"

"Best of luck and keep your head down," Stotz says.

"Watch out for toasters," Joe adds, and the man looks puzzled but not unhappy with that. He gives them a thumbs-up and disappears back out into the hall.

It all still seems pointless. Toledo is still a disaster, Columbus is becoming one, and if you asked each one of the soldiers going out the door what they were fighting for, he's not sure most of them could answer, but Joe knows for certain that some battlefields are easier to walk off of than others.

Stotz tosses him the brush, then holds up a datachip, the latest incoming program set from central dining services. "Wanna see how bad they screwed up Mac & Cheese?" he asks.

[CC] Welcome online, Autonomous Spleen Replacement Unit Model 448-G9. This is your introductory Initial Boot orientation. I am Cybernetic Cerebral Control and Delegation Implant Module CI4210-A. I respond to CC—

[SPLEEN::UNIT2] Hello! I'm happy to be here! I am eager to receive your exspleenation of our present circumstances. Do you get it? Ex*splee*—

[CC] New Spleen, you should be aware that—

[SPLEEN::UNIT2] . . . that it's spleendid to meet me? Why thank you!

[HEART] Ah bloody hell. I miss old Spleen already.

ABOUT THE AUTHOR

Suzanne Palmer is a writer and linux system administrator who lives in western Massachusetts. Her work has appeared frequently in *Asimov's* and *Analog*, and her *Clarkesworld* story "The Secret Life of Bots" won the 2018 Hugo for Best Novelette. Her first novel, "Finder", comes out from DAW in April 2018.

In Everlasting Wisdom

ALIETTE DE BODARD

The path to enlightenment is through obedience to wisdom, and who is wiser than the Everlasting Emperor?

It's the words that keep Ai Thi going, day after day—the ceaseless flow of wisdom from the appeaser within her, reminders that the Everlasting Emperor loves her and her sacrifice—that she's doing her duty, day after day, making sure that nothing discordant or dissident can mar the harmony that keeps the Empire together.

Her daily rounds take her through the Inner Rings of Vermillion Crab Station: she sits on the train, head lolled back against the window, thinking of nothing in particular as the appeaser does their work, sending the Everlasting Emperor's words into passengers' subconscious minds. Ai Thi sees the words take root: the tension leaves the air, the tautness of people's worries and anger drains out of them, and they relax, faces slack, eyes closed, all thoughts in perfect harmony. The appeaser shifts and twists within Ai Thi, a familiar rhythm of little bubbles in her gut, almost as if she were pregnant with her daughter Dieu Kiem again.

The worst enemy is the enemy within, because it could wear the face of your brother or mother.

Loyalty to the Everlasting Emperor should be stronger than the worship offered to ancestors, or the respect afforded to parents.

The words aren't meant for Ai Thi: they go through her like running water, from the appeaser to her to the passengers on the train. She's the bridge—the appeaser is lodged within her, but they're an alien being and need Ai Thi and her fellow harmonizers to speak the proper language, to teach them the proper words.

Ai Thi knows all the words. Once, they were the only thing that kept her going.

It is the duty of children to die for their parents, and the duty of all subjects to give their life for the Everlasting Emperor—though he never asks for more than what is necessary, and reasonably borne.

Ai Thi has only confused, jumbled memories of her implantation—a white, sterilized room that smells of disinfectant; the smooth voice of doctors and nurses, telling her to lie down on the operating table, that everything will be fine. She woke up with her voice scraped raw, as if she'd screamed for hours; with memories of struggling against restraints—but when she looked at her wrists and ankles, there was no trace of anything, not a single abrasion. And, later, alone in her room, a single, horrifying recollection: asking about painkillers and the doctors shaking their heads, telling her she had to endure it all without help, because analgesics were poison to the appeaser's metabolism.

Her roommate Lan says that they do give drugs—something to make the harmonizers forget the pain, the hours spent raving and twisting and screaming while the appeasers burrow into their guts.

It's all absurd, of course. It must be false impressions brought on by the drugs and the procedure, for why would the Everlasting Emperor take such bad care of those that serve him?

Ai Thi remembers waking up at night after the implantation, shivering and shaking with a terrible hunger—she was alone in the darkness, small and insignificant, and she could call for help but she didn't matter—the doctors had gone home and no one would come, no one remembered she was there. Around her, the shadows of the room seemed to twist and come alive—if she turned and looked away, they would swallow her whole, crush her until nothing was left. She reached for the rice cakes on the table—and they slid into her stomach, as thin and as tasteless as paper, doing nothing to assuage the hunger. Empty, she was empty, and nothing would ever fill that hole within her . . .

Not her hunger. Not her loneliness. The appeaser's. Cut off from the communion of their own kind, they so desperately needed contact to live, so desperately craved warmth and love.

You're not alone, Ai Thi whispered. *You are a subject of the Everlasting Emperor, and he loves you as a father loves his children.*

You're not alone.

Night after night, telling them the words from her training, the ones endlessly welling up out of her, like blood out of a wound. *The Everlasting Emperor was human once, but he transcended that condition. He knows all our weaknesses, and he watches over us all. He asks only for respect and obedience in return for endless love.*

You—we are part of something so much greater than ourselves: an Empire that has always been, that will always be as timeless as the Heavens. Through us—through the work of hundreds, of thousands like us, it will endure into this generation, and into the next.

Night after night, until the words became part of the appeaser—burrowed into them as they had burrowed within Ai Thi's guts—until they ceaselessly spoke in her sleep, giving her back her own words with unwavering strength.

Beware what you read. The Quynh Federation reaches everywhere, to disseminate their lies: you cannot trust news that hasn't been vetted.

Ai Thi gets down at her usual station: White Crane Monastery, close to the barracks. She has one last quadrant to go through on her rounds, Eggshell Celadon, making sure that the families there understand the cost of war fought beyond the Empire's boundaries, and the necessity of the war effort.

As she turns into a corridor decorated with a splash of stars, she hears the footsteps behind her. A menial, going to work—a kitchen hand, like Ai Thi used to be before she volunteered—or a sweeper, supervising bots as they clean the quadrant. But at the next corridor—one that holds the machinery of the station rather than cramped family compartments—the footsteps are still here.

She turns, briefly, catching a glimpse of hempen clothes, torn sleeves, and the glint of metal. From the appeaser, a vague guess that whoever it is is determined: the appeaser can't read human thoughts, can't interpret them, or the harmonizers' and enforcers' work would be that much simpler. What they know from human behavior, they learned from Ai Thi.

Captain Giang's advice to her trainees: always choose the ground for a confrontation, rather than having choice forced on you.

Ai Thi stops, at the middle of the corridor—no nooks or crannies, no alcoves where her pursuer can hide. Within her the appeaser is silent and still, trying to find the proper words of the Everlasting Emperor for the circumstances, gathering strength for a psychic onslaught.

She's expected a group of dissidents—Sergeant Bac said they were getting bolder in the daily briefing—but it's just one person.

A woman in shapeless bot-milled clothes, bottom of the range—face gaunt, eyes sunken deep, lips so thin they look like the slash of a knife. Her hands rests inside her sleeves, fingers bunched. She has a knife or a gun. "Harmonizer," the woman whispers. "How can you—how can you—"

Ai Thi spreads her hands, to show that she is unarmed; though it isn't true. The appeaser is her best and surest weapon, but only used at the proper time. "I serve the Everlasting Emperor."

The woman doesn't answer. She merely quickens her pace. Her hand swings out, and it's a gun that she holds, the barrel glinting in the station's light, running towards Ai Thi and struggling to aim.

No time.

Ai Thi picks one saying, one piece of wisdom, from all the ones swarming in her mind. *The Everlasting Emperor loves all his subjects like children, and it is the duty of children to bow down to their parents.*

Bow down.

And she lets the appeaser hurl it like a thrown stone, straight into the woman's thoughts. No subtlety, not the usual quiet influence, the background to everyone's daily lives—just a noise that overwhelms everything like a scream.

Bow down.

The woman falters, even as her gun locks into place: there's a sound like thunder—Ai Thi throws herself to the side, momentarily deafened—comes up for breath, finding herself still alive, the appeaser within her driving her on.

Bow down.

She reaches the woman, twists a wrist that has gone limp. The gun clatters to the ground. That's the only sound in the growing silence—that, and the woman's ragged breath. The appeaser within Ai Thi relaxes, slightly. She can feel their disapproval, their fear. Cutting it too close. She could have died. *They* could have died.

Ai Thi lifts the woman to her feet, effortlessly. "You shouldn't have done this," she says. "Who sent you?"

She hasn't expected an answer—the woman's mind should still be filled with the single message the appeaser used to drown all cognitive function—but the thin, pale lips part. "I sent myself. You—you starve us, and expect us to smile."

"We all sacrifice things. It's the price to pay for safety," Ai Thi says, automatically, and then takes another look at the woman. All skin and bones—Ai Thi is strong from training, but the woman hardly weighs anything, and her cheeks are far gaunter than even those of menials—and, as she looks into the woman's eyes, she sees nothing but raw, naked desperation, an expression she knows all too well.

Who sent you?

I sent myself.

Two years ago, an eternity ago, Ai Thi looked at that same gaze in the mirror, working herself down to the bone for not enough money, not enough food, going to bed hungry every night and listening to Dieu Kiem's hacking cough, and knowing that no doctor would tend to the poor and desperate. She made a choice, then: she volunteered for implantation, knowing she might not survive it—volunteered to serve the Everlasting Emperor in spite of her doubts. But, if she hadn't made that choice—if she'd let fear and frustration and hunger whittle her down to red-hot rage—

This might have been her, with a gun.

Ai Thi is meant to call for the enforcers, to turn the woman over to them for questioning, so that they can track down and break the dissident cell or foreign agency that sent her. That would be the loyal, righteous thing to do. But . . .

But she's been here. She knows there's no cell—merely the end of a road; a last, desperate gesture that, if it doesn't succeed, will at least end everything.

Ai Thi walks back to the barracks with the woman over her shoulder—by then she's all spent, and lies in Ai Thi's grip like wrung cloth. Ai Thi lays her down in an alcove before the entrance, a little out of sight. "Wait here," she says.

By the time Ai Thi comes back, she half expects the woman to be gone. But she's still there, waiting—she sits on the floor with her legs drawn against her, huddling as though it might make her smaller.

"Here," Ai Thi says. She grabbed what she could from the refectory—couldn't dally, or she'd be noticed: two small rice cakes, and a handful of cotton fish.

The woman looks at her, warily; snatches all three things out of her hand.

"Go gently, or you'll just vomit it." Ai Thi crouches, watching her. The appeaser within her is quiet. Curious. "It's not poisoned."

The woman's laugh is short, and unamused. "I didn't think it was." She nibbles, cautiously, at the rice cakes; eating half of one before she slips the rest inside her sleeves.

"What's your name?"

A hesitation, then: "Hien Hoa. You'd find out, anyway."

"I don't have supernatural powers," Ai Thi says, mildly.

"No, but you have the powers of the state." Hoa stops, then; afraid she's gone too far.

Ai Thi shakes her head. "I'm not going to turn you in. I'd have done it already, if I was."

"Why—"

Ai Thi shrugs, though she doesn't quite know what to say. "Everyone deserves a second chance, I guess." She rises, ignoring the twinges of pain in her muscles. "Stay out of trouble, will you? I'd hate to see someone else bring you in."

Straying from the Everlasting Emperor's path is a grievous misconduct, but every misconduct can be atoned for—every fault can be forgiven, if the proper amends are made, the proper reeducation achieved.

To Sergeant Bac, at her debriefing in the squad room, Ai Thi says nothing of Hoa. She heads next to Captain Giang's office, for her weekly interview.

The captain sits behind her desk, staring at the aggregated reports of her company, nodding, from time to time, at something that pleases or bothers her. On the desk before her is a simple *am* and *duong* logo, a half-black, half-white circle curved in the shape of an appeaser: the emblem of the harmonizers "I see your last checkup was three months ago," she says.

Ai Thi nods.

"You're well, I trust?" Captain Giang says—only half a question. "No stomach pains. No headaches that won't go away. No blood in your urine."

The danger symptoms—the ones Ai Thi could recite by heart—a sign that the delicate symbiosis that links her and the appeaser is out of kilter, and that they could both die. "I . . . I don't think so," Ai Thi says.

Giang looks at her, for a while. "You don't look like yourself," she says, frowning.

She knows. No. There is no way she can know. Ai Thi draws a deep, ragged breath. "There's much unease," she says, finally, a half-truth. "People are . . . taut. Like a string about to snap." And there is only so much slack the harmonizers can pick up, only so much wisdom they can dispense to people whose only thoughts and worries are what they'll be eating come tomorrow.

"I see. Why do you think that is?"

Gaunt eyes, and Hoa's thin, bruised lips, and the careful way she's hoarded the food; for giving to someone else. Ai Thi says, finally, "May I speak freely?"

"Always." Giang frowns. "This isn't a jail or a reeducation camp. We trust your loyalty."

Of course they do, and of course they can. Ai Thi would never do anything against the Everlasting Emperor: he keeps the fabric of society together. "The war effort against the Quynh Federation is costly. Food is more and more expensive, and this creates . . . anger. Jealousy. They think the soldiers favored." And the harmonizers, and the enforcers, and the scholars that keep the machinery of the Empire going.

Giang doesn't speak, for a while. Her broad face is emotionless. "They would," she says. "But the soldiers pay dearly for that food. People on the station aren't at risk of losing limbs or pieces of their mind, or being tortured for information on the Empire." Ai Thi can feel, distantly, Giang's own appeaser, a thin thread at the back of her mind, whispering about love and need and duty, all the sayings she already knows by heart.

She says, "I know this."

"And they don't?" Giang sighs. "I'm not questioning your conclusions, private. But as you know, the war isn't going well. The Everlasting Emperor is going to announce an increase of the war effort."

"You said the soldiers paid for the food because they were at greater risk. But we—" Ai Thi says.

Giang raises an eyebrow. "Are we not?" Her gaze is sardonic, and Ai Thi remembers Hoa's gun going off, the thunder filling her ears. "We'll be the first against the wall, if things do break down." It sounds like a warning, though Ai Thi isn't sure who she means it for.

Perhaps us, the appeaser whispers, but they barely sound worried. Only about Hoa, which surprises Ai Thi; but of course they would know all about hunger and need.

"There's much unrest," Giang says. "I don't want you to patrol in pairs—you cover less ground—but it might become necessary. Private Khanh was attacked by a group of three dissidents masquerading as beggars, and only barely escaped."

"Is he—" Ai Thi asks, but Giang shook her head.

"He's fine. We didn't manage to catch them, though." Giang sounds annoyed. "Cinnabar Mansions Quadrant reported two riots in as many weeks. As you said, people are wound taut."

"But we'll be fine," Ai Thi says, before she can think.

"Of course we will. The Empire has weathered wars and fire and riots long before we were both born," Giang says. She makes a gesture with her hands. "Dismissed, private. Enjoy your rest."

It's only after Ai Thi has left the office, halfway to her room and the light comedy vid she was looking forward to, that she realizes that the warm feeling of utter certainty within her is from Giang's appeaser.

The foundations of the Everlasting Empire: the censors, rooting out disinformation from vids and newscasts. The scholars, making the laws everyone must abide by. The harmonizers and enforcers, keeping the fabric of the Empire clear of dissidence. And the soldiers, defending the borders against enemy incursions.

"There's someone at the gates asking after you, lil sis," Lan says. She laughs, throwing her head back in a gesture so familiar it's barely annoying anymore. "A menial. From your old life?"

Lan comes from the Inner Rings, the wealthiest Station inhabitants. She caused some scandal at an examination, and her family gave her the choice of enlisting with the harmonizers, or with the soldiers on the front. She's Ai Thi's roommate, and she means well, but sometimes her assumptions about people grate. To wit: Ai Thi didn't keep contact with anyone from her old workplaces—such attachments aren't encouraged, in any case.

It can't be Second Aunt, because Ai Thi is currently in communication with home, and spoke to her not a minute past. "Can you ask them to wait?" Ai Thi says. Her time for outside calls is almost up, in any case. She turns back to Dieu Kiem. "Sorry. Duty calling."

Her daughter makes a grimace in her field of vision. She's a ghostly overlay in Ai Thi's implants, a tall and willowy girl who seems to have shot up three heads since Ai Thi was last given a permission home. "Captain Giang." She looks as though she's about to laugh. "Fine, but can you tell Great Aunt I want the network key?"

Ai Thi purses her lips. "She told me you hacked it and had every wall display copies of Huong Trang's poems. The more explicit ones."

"As practice," Dieu Kiem snorts. "Too easy."

She's growing up too fast, too strong. Ai Thi wants to tell her to be careful, but there's nothing illegal or reprehensible in what she's doing—just harmless pranks, the kind even the Everlasting Emperor would smile upon. But where does dissidence start?

She has no answer. She logs off in spite of Dieu Kiem's complaints, promising her that she'll have a word with Second Aunt—wondering, once again, how time passes, how little she sees of her own daughter.

Sacrifices aren't necessary, but they are all the more valued when they do occur.

The appeaser within her is . . . sad? There's a peculiar tautness in her mind, as if the entire world were about to come apart. She understands that they're sad, too, grieving for time lost.

"Thank you," she says, aloud, shaking her head. "But it's nothing we can't survive."

Warmth from within her; a sated need. The appeaser curls back to their usual, watchful self, chewing on sayings and wisdom they might need for their next patrol.

Outside the gates, Hoa is waiting for her. Ai Thi fights off the urge to pinch herself. "I didn't think—"

"That I'd come back?" Hoa is still gaunt and pale, but there's a light in her eyes that wasn't there before. Ai Thi is afraid to ask where it comes from, but Hoa merely shakes her head. "I found a second job." She grins, waving a basket towards Ai Thi. "And I owe you a meal."

They walk towards a nearby white space in silence. Ai Thi reaches out, deftly shaping a small corner of it into a lush green space, like the jungles in the stories of her childhood. Hoa sits down at the foot of a huge fig tree, setting down the basket between ghostly roots—Ai Thi hasn't reshaped reality, merely added a layer of illusion that they share across their implants.

Inside the basket are four puffed-up dough pieces, and grilled maize. Hoa hands them out, grimacing. "I wasn't sure if—" she pauses, embarrassed—"if you ate more."

Ai Thi guesses the unsaid words. "Because of the appeaser? A little, but not much." It's not like being pregnant. The appeaser is small, and will never grow within her: they have already had their children, the next generation of appeasers raised in tanks for implantation in the next generation of trainees.

They eat the first fried dough piece in silence, not quite sure what to say to each other. Ai Thi doesn't know why Hoa came back. She says, finally, "I saw you take the rice cakes. You have a family?"

Hoa looks at her for a while. "I thought you knew everything."

Ai Thi laughs. "I wish. But no. I'm not the Census Office."

"A toddler," Hoa says. "Three years old."

"Mine is older," Ai Thi says, with a sigh. "Thirteen years old and all opinions." She's not sure why she says, "I almost never see her. Duty."

Hoa laughs, a little sadly. It doesn't sound strained or forced, though the atmosphere is still tense. "You're different."

"From other harmonizers?" Ai Thi shrugs, and finally speaks the truth. "I was where you are, once. Working in a restaurant in the daytime, and cleaning the corridors at night. Starving myself to feed my child."

Hoa is staring at her. "That's why you became a harmonizer? For money?" There is . . . an edge to her voice, a hint of disapproval that's not meant to exist. Captain Giang is right. The fabric of society is fraying.

"Because I had nowhere else to go," Ai Thi says, simply. "Because . . . because I listened to the voice of the Everlasting Emperor, and he gave me a second chance."

"You've never seen him," Hoa says. A question, a challenge.

"Once," Ai Thi says. She doesn't need to close her eyes to remember. She was standing at the back of the harmonizers' ranks, and even from there she felt the radiance of his presence, wave after wave of warmth filling her, the world wavering and bending until it was all she could do not to fall on her knees. "He was everything they say he was, and more."

Hoa is silent, for a while. "Faith," she says, and her voice is full of wonder. "I thought—" she shakes her head. "I suppose it takes a lot, to get implanted. May I—" Her hand reaches out, resting close to Ai Thi's torso.

Ai Thi nods. Hoa's fingers rest on her gut, pressing down, lightly. The appeaser gurgles within her—kicks towards Hoa, who withdraws as if burned. The appeaser's disappointment burns in Ai Thi like acid, spreading outwards through the only channel they know how to use.

Before the Everlasting Emperor, all citizens are weighed equally: the only thing that matters is their loyalty.

Hoa takes one, two steps backwards, her face twisting as the full blast of emotions hits her. "What—"

"They're hurt," Ai Thi says. "Because you think they're less than human."

Hoa opens her mouth. She's going to say that of course they're not human, that they're just an alien parasite, and all the insults Ai Thi has had hurled at her by dissidents. Ai Thi cuts her off before she can speak, "They're lonely. Always lonely. That's the price they pay for service to the Everlasting Emperor."

Hoa closes her mouth. Her face goes through contortions. "I'm sorry." And she kneels, hand held out, making it clear that it's not to Ai Thi she's apologizing.

Warmth spreading through Ai Thi—the appeaser. They like her.

Hoa reaches out, holds out a piece of dough again. "Hungry?" she asks.

Ai Thi eats it. It feels sweeter than honey as it slides down her throat, the appeaser's approval a small sun within her, spreading to all her limbs—an odd, unsettling, but welcome feeling.

At length, Hoa speaks, again. "So they're starving you, too."

Ai Thi shakes her head. "I don't understand—"

"Of love and kin and warmth." Hoa's voice is sad. "Hollowing you out, and leaving nothing but words."

Ai Thi wants to say something about wisdom, about the Everlasting Emperor, about necessary sacrifices, but the words seem to shrivel in her mouth. Hoa's burning eyes hold her—the same desperate need she saw in them, back when she almost arrested her, except that it's . . . pity?

"I'm sorry. You shouldn't be doing this to yourself," Hoa says again, and it *is* pity. Compassion. She doesn't understand, she doesn't see how much the Everlasting Emperor keeps Ai Thi going, doesn't understand how much the words mean, how they keep the world together—except that Dieu Kiem is growing up without her, and all that Ai Thi can remember is the appeaser's desperate, lonely hunger, a bottomless well that nothing can ever fill . . .

She's up, and running away from the park before she can think, heedless to Hoa's calls. She only stops when she gets to her room, breathing hard and feeling as though the air she inhales never reaches her burning lungs.

The Everlasting Emperor has always been, and will always be. The Empire is as long-lasting as the stars in the heavens. As long as the bonds between mother and daughter, between brother and brother endure, then it, too, shall.

There's a noise outside like the roar of the sea. Ai Thi wakes up, and the sound swells to fill her entire universe. "Mother? Mother?"

Dieu Kiem, through her implants. "Child. How did you—"

Her daughter's voice is tight, on the verge of panic. "Hacked your coms. That's not the point. Mother, you need to move. They say there are riots all over the station."

What—how? Ai Thi fumbles, trying to find something solid—she rubs a hand on her guts, feeling the reassuring mass of the appeaser within her. "Child? Child?"

Dieu Kiem's voice comes in fast, words jumbled together. "The Everlasting Emperor ordered the closure of half the granaries across all quadrants. An enforcer shot someone, and then—"

"Closure. Why? For the war effort?" Ai Thi asks, but there's no answer. Nothing but silence on the coms now, but the roar is still there, and she knows it's that of a crowd massed at the gates. She could call up the outside cameras on her implants, but there's no point.

It's night in the barracks. Lan is on patrol—should be, if she wasn't caught in the riots. Ai Thi has known for a while that things are taut, but for riots to be this widespread, this fast? Things are bad. Very bad. Ai Thi hits the general alert on the network. She heads to the squad room first, but it's deserted and silent—and shifts course, to get to Giang's office.

She finds the Captain putting on her jacket, straightening her official rank patch on her chest, the eyes of the tiger shining in the dim light. "Captain—"

"I know." Giang's voice is curt.

Mankind is but one step away from lawlessness. Only the word of Heaven and of the Everlasting Emperor keeps us from becoming monsters to one another.

Barely contained panic within Ai Thi—Giang's appeaser, not hers—hers is silent and watchful, but not surprised.

"We have to hold," Captain Giang says. "We need to reestablish harmony and order." She shakes her head. Again that feeling of rising panic within Ai Thi, the edge of something so strong Giang can barely contain it.

"Captain—"

Giang is halfway to the door already. "There's no time, private. Come."

Something is wrong. Not the riot, not the crowd, not what seems like a station-wide panic. Captain Giang wouldn't lose her head over that. And she's not currently broadcasting emotions at Ai Thi. Whatever causes that panic is so strong that it's simply spilling outwards, like the hurt of Ai Thi's appeaser when Hoa wouldn't touch them.

And why hasn't she mentioned reinforcements? "Captain," Ai Thi says, again. "We'll hold, but what about Plum Blossom Company?"

Giang turns then. For a moment, her composure breaks, and the face she shows to Ai Thi is the white, ashen one of a corpse, a bewildered, lost, and hungry ghost. "The dissidents have overwhelmed the Palace of Heaven and Earth, private. The Everlasting Emperor is dead."

Dead.

No.

The roar in Ai Thi's ears isn't the sound of the crowd—it's a long, desperate scream that scrapes her throat raw, and she can't tell if it's coming from her or the appeaser.

"How can he—" she starts, stops, unable to voice the enormity of it. "How—"

Giang has pulled herself together again. "I don't know," she says. "But that's not what matters. There are no reinforcements coming, private."

Outside, on Ai Thi's implants, the crowd has trampled the two harmonizers guarding the gates. A press of people is battering at the gates, and it's only a matter of time until the fragile metal gives way.

Dead.

The Empire is as long-lasting as the stars in the heavens, as the bonds of filial duty between parents and children.

The Empire . . .

They'll die, holding the barracks. Die trying to impose harmony on a crowd that's too large and too big for them to control.

"Captain, we can't—"

"I know we can't hold." Giang is at the door: she doesn't turn around anymore. Ai Thi calls up the inside of the gates on her implants, sees another press: Kim Cuc and Tuyet and Vu and half the harmonizers in the barracks in a loose formation that mixes all squads under the orders of Sergeant Bac and Sergeant Hong, sending wave after wave of appeaser thoughts towards the crowd, trying to calm them down. It's like throwing stones and hoping to stop the ocean.

Giang says, "We swore an oath to the Emperor, private. Loyalty unto death."

Giang's appeaser: warmth and contentment within Ai Thi, the satisfaction of duty done to the bitter end. *It is the duty of all subjects to give their life . . .*

Within Ai Thi, her appeaser stirs—brings up, not the Everlasting Emperor's voice, but Hoa's compassion-filled gaze, Hoa's voice, a rock against which the other appeaser's thoughts shatter.

You shouldn't be doing this to yourself.

"It's not . . . " Ai Thi says. She's surprised at how steady her voice sounds.

"I beg your pardon?" Giang stops then.

"It's not our duty," Ai Thi says. "That's not how that saying ends, Captain."

He never asks for more than what is necessary, and reasonably borne.

The Everlasting Emperor is dead. There is nothing that says they have to die, too.

Ai Thi's appeaser has fallen silent, knowing exactly what she wants. She feels the thoughts from Giang's appeaser, dancing on the edge of her mind—duty, loyalty, death, a trembling wall she can barely hold at bay for long.

Giang moves back into her office, comes to stand before her. "This isn't a discussion, private. It's an order."

Necessary. Reasonably borne. Ai Thi uncoils, then—even as, within her, the appeaser moves—a psychic onslaught centered around a single, pinpoint thought. Giang grunts, goes down on one knee, eyes rolling up in her face, and Ai Thi's hand strikes her jugular, taking her down.

Ai Thi stands, breathing hard, over Giang's unconscious body—for a moment, at a loss at what she's done, what she should do—but there is only one thing that she can do, after all. The rioters will come for their families next, and neither Second Aunt nor Dieu Kiem have had any training in combat or eluding pursuers. There's a risk she'll lead the crowd straight to them, but it's offset by what she and the appeaser can bring them. She can help. She has to.

Ai Thi thinks of the other harmonizers, lined against the doors and waiting for them to cave in. She heads towards the squad room. Within her, rising emptiness, a howling need—how will they survive, with the Everlasting Emperor dead—what does wisdom mean, anymore, if its incarnation is no more—nothing, there is nothing left . . .

In the squad room, there's only Lan, bloodied and out of breath, who smiles grimly at her. "It's a war zone out there. Fortunately they haven't found the back door yet, but I don't know how long we can hold."

Ai Thi's voice comes from very far away—a stranger's, utterly emotionless—because the alternative would be an endless scream. "The Everlasting Emperor is dead. Captain Giang . . . says to run. To scatter back to our families. There's no point in holding. We've already lost."

They've lost everything. They—

For a long, agonizingly long moment, Lan stares at her—as if she knew, as if she could read straight into Ai Thi's mind. She smiles again, almost with fondness. "Families. Of course."

Her hand rests, lightly, on Ai Thi's shoulder, squeezes once, twice. "I'll tell them, though not everyone will listen. But you run, lil sis."

And then she's gone, and it's just Ai Thi, walking through empty corridors towards the back of the barracks, the roar of the crowd receding into meaninglessness.

It's not too late. She can go out of the barracks—go back the way Lan came from—go get her aunt and daughter before the rioters find new targets—she can run, as fiercely, as far away as she can—to the heart of the Quynh Federation if need be. They can make a new life, one that's no longer in service to the Everlasting Emperor.

They can—

The Emperor is dead, and nothing will ever be right again—the appeaser reaching, again and again, for words, remembering that they mean nothing now.

"Ssh," Ai Thi says, aloud, to the appeaser. "It'll be all right. It's nothing we can't survive." And, slowly, gently, sings the lullabies she used to sing to Dieu Kiem when she was a child—again and again as they both run from the shadow of the barracks—again and again until the songs fill the hollow, wordless silence within her.

Originally published in *Infinity Wars,* edited by Jonathan Strahan.

ABOUT THE AUTHOR

Aliette de Bodard writes speculative fiction: her short stories have garnered her two Nebula Awards, a Locus Award, and two British Science Fiction Association Awards. She is the author of the Dominion of the Fallen series, set in a turn-of-the-century Paris devastated by a magical war, which comprises *The House of Shattered Wings* (2015 British Science Fiction Association Award, Locus Award finalist), and its standalone sequel *The House of Binding Thorns* (Ace, Gollancz, 2017 European Science Fiction Society Achievement Award). Her most recent book is *In the Vanishers' Palace,* a dark retelling of Beauty and the Beast where they are both women and the Beast is a dragon. She lives in Paris.

The Falls: A Luna Story

IAN MCDONALD

My daughter fell from the top of the world. She tripped, she gripped, she slipped, and she fell. Into three kilometers of open air.

I have a desk. Everyone on the atmospheric entry project thinks it's the quaintest thing. They can't understand it. Look at the space it takes up! And it attracts stuff. Junk. Piles. De-print them, de-print it, get rid of the dust, free up the space. Surfaces. You don't need surfaces to work.

That's true. I work through Marid, my familiar. I've skinned it as its namesake, a great and powerful Dijon, hovering over my left shoulder. My coworkers think this quaint too. I spend my shifts in a pavilion of interlocutors. My familiar meeting my client's familiar: relaying each other's words.

My client is a planetary exploration probe.

I'm a simulational psychiatrist.

The proper furniture of psychologist is a chair, not a cluttered desk. And a couch. To which I say; the couch is a psychoanalytic cliché, and try laying a Saturn entry probe on a chaise lounge, even before you get to the Oedipal rage and penis envy. The desk stays. Yes it takes up stupid space in my office, yes, I have piled it with so many empty food containers and disposable teacups and kawaii toys and even physical printouts that I'm permanently running close to my carbon limit. But I like it, it makes this cubicle an office. And it displays—displayed, before the strata of professional detritus buried it—my daughter's first archaeological find.

The technology is awkward by our standards—silicon microprocessor arrays are like asteroids next to modern 2-D graphene films; almost laughable. A finger-sized processor board; its exact purpose unknown. Its provenance: the location where the People's Republic of China's Yutu rover came to a halt and died forty kilometers south of Laplace F in the Mare Imbrium on the nearside of the Moon.

Acceleration under gravity on the surface of the Moon is 1.625 meters per second squared.

I like Callisto.

I don't like—I don't have to like—all my clients. Every AI is different, though there are similarities, some of them the constraints of their architecture and engineering, some of them philosophical, some of them the shared AI culture that has been evolving on the Moon alongside human society. Every AI is an individual, not an identity.

Callisto is quick, keen and erudite in conversation, charmingly pedantic, eager and naïve. E anticipates the mission with the impatience and excitement of a child going to New Year and there is the trap. I think of er like Shahina, and then I'm making mistakes. I become attached, I make presumptions. I *humanize.*

Erm, Nuur did you see what you did there?

"I beg your pardon Callisto?"

Erm, you used a wrong word.

"What wrong word?"

I can remind you . . .

"Please do. I hate to think I'd said something inappropriate."

You said, talking about my atmospheric entry aspect, when she *goes in. I think you meant to say . . .*

E. Er. The recognized pronouns for Artificial Intelligence. My embarrassment was crippling. I couldn't speak. I blushed, burned. Burbled apologies. I was naked with shame.

It's quite all right, Nuur. But I think I should tell you that you've, um, been doing it all week . . .

When an AI ums, ers, demurs, it is a clear sign of a conflict between its laws: to be truthful, to cause no harm to humans. AIs are every bit as shy and self-deluding as humans.

I didn't laugh when she said, *history*. I didn't smile, didn't interject, object, reject, though the arguments swarmed on my tongue. This is the Moon. Our society is fifty years old, it's a century-and-some since we first walked here. We are five cities, a university, a clutter of habitats and bases and one ever-moving train-cum-refinery; one million seven hundred thousand people. How can we have a history? How much does it take to have a history as opposed to anecdotes? Is there a critical mass? We are renter-clients of the Lunar Development Corporation, employed or contracted by the Five Dragons; history, for us, is over. We work, we survive, we pay our per diems for the Four Elementals of Air, Water, Data, Carbon. We don't just not need history; we can't afford history. Where is the profit? Where is the utility? So quick, so easy, see? I talk for a living. Arguments come to me as if drawn by whispers and pheromones. But I pushed them behind me and spoke none of them.

History, she said, spying the shadows of all those arguments and disparagements behind me. Defying me to criticize. *We have a history. Everything has a history. History isn't a thing you find lying around, it's a thing you make.*

Shahina, I named her. The name means falcon: a small fierce beautiful quick bird. She has never seen a falcon, never seen a bird, never seen a winged thing that isn't human, apart from the butterfly-fountains AKA make for society parties; that only live for a day and clog the drains when they make it rain to clear the dust from the air.

I have never seen a falcon either, for that matter. My father kept pigeons in a loft in the shade of the solar panel. I never liked them; they were smelly and rattly and jabby and swarmed around me when I went up on the roof with my Dad to feed them. Their wings clattered; they seemed more machine than bird. The thought of them now, cities, countries, worlds distant, still raises a cold horror. Falcons are the enemies of pigeons; Dad kept an evil eye for their swooshes in the sky. They're moving into the city, he said. Nesting up in the new towers. To them it's just a glass cliff. Any shadow he didn't like the look of was a falcon.

Shahina has never seen a falcon, never seen a bird, never seen a sky. But she's well-named. She is so quick. Her thoughts swerve and dodge, nimble and swift. Mine plod in slow, straight lines. She rushes to opinions and positions as if fortifying a hill. My work is deliberate: the identification and engineering of artificial emotions. She is fierce. Those opinions, those positions she defends with a ferocity that beats down any possible opposition. She wins not by being right but by being vehemently wrong. She scares me, when we fight as mother and daughter do. She scares me away from arguing.

History: what is it good for?

So, a thing can only be good if it's for *something?* she snapped back.

But are there jobs; will it pay your Four Elementals?

So, education is really just apprenticeship?

What's there to study? All we have are contracts.

Don't you get it? The contracts are the history.

And she would toss back her long, so shiny curls to show her exasperation that I would never ever understand *anything*, and let it settle under the slow lunar gravity.

Quick, fierce, but not small. I've been twenty years on the Moon and it's turned me lean and scrawny, top heavy and bandy legged; tall and thin but Shahina towers over me. She is lunar-born, a second generation. Moon-kid. She is as lean and elegant as a gazelle.

I felt small and frail as a sparrow, hugging her goodbye at the station.

Why does it have to be Meridian?

I couldn't help myself.

I saw my daughter's eyes widen in the moment before the *this-again* roll, her lips tighten. She drew back from the edge of fierce.

It's the best History Colloquium. And anyway, I always wanted to see the Earth.

She bent down to kiss me and then went through the pressure gate to the train.

At Farside Station that day were some third-gens. They overbore Shahina and her generation as she overbore me. Alien children.

Mean atmospheric pressure inside lunar habitats is 1060 kilopascals, significantly higher than terrestrial norm.

I hover, Shahina told me. Over her, from the other side of the Moon. There's guilt first, when your daughter finds out you've been spying on her, then shame that you were so easily detected, then outrage at her outrage: it's only because I care, I shouldn't worry but I can't help myself; it's so far away. I'm worried about you. Doesn't she know it's only because I care?

The first time I went to Meridian to visit Shahina I saw an angel. I've lived all my life in the university, its cramped cloisters and mean halls, in the settlements of Farside, small and widely scattered, across many amors and amories. I turned my back on Earth and never looked over my shoulder. In those years away from the face of the Earth, looking out into deep space, the great nearside cities have delved deep and wide, quadras opened and linked into stupendous, vertiginous chasms, glittering at night with thousands of lights. They sent quaint, tight-horizoned me dizzy with agoraphobia. I caught hold of Shahina's arm as we came up out of Meridian Station. I felt old and infirm. I'm neither. Shahina sat me on a bench under the cover of trees, beneath leaves so that the lights became stars, half-seen. She bought me sherbet ice from an AKA tricycle and it was then that I saw the angel. People fly on the

Moon, I've known that forever, even before I came here and made it my home. It's the sole comprehensible image of life on the Moon to terrestrials: the soaring winged woman. Always a woman. Dizzy, I heard a movement, a rustle, a displacement of air. I looked up in time to see wings flicker over me, lights moving against the higher constellations. A woman, rigged with navigation lights, flying. She stooped down across the treetops, shadow, movement, sparkles glimpsed through the leaves. I looked up, our faces met. Then she beat her wings and pulled up out of her glide, climbing, twisting in helical flight until she was lost to my view, her lesser lights merging with the greater.

"Oh," I said. And, "Did you . . . "

"Yes, mum."

I thought about the flying woman, that moment of elements meeting, over the following days as Shahina introduced me, one by one, to her circle. Friends, colleagues, Colloquium fellows. Sergei her tall, polite amor. He was an archaeologist. I terrified him by existing. I wondered what Shahina had told him about me. They cooked for me. It was so special and touching. They had hired hob and utensils, plates and chopsticks. They had obviously rehearsed, their movements in the tiny kitchen area of the Colloquium apt—cramped even by Farside U standards—was as immaculately choreographed as a ballet.

"Archaeology?"

I saw a flicker of impatience, a twitch of irritation before Sergei answered me.

"We've been living here for fifty years. It's been a century since the first human landing, over a hundred years since the first probes hard-landed. That's deep enough for archaeology."

"I get this from studying history," Shahina said and she rested her hand on Sergei's. She was trying to softly intervene, to ameliorate, but I had no ill will to Sergei. I had neither ill will nor affection for him. He seemed a serious, flavorless boy, kind but dull. I could not understand what my daughter saw in him. I was neither surprised nor disappointed that it didn't last. Nor was Shahina, I think.

Shahina waited until I was on the platform, the train sliding in behind the glass pressure wall, before giving me the gift. It was small, the size of my thumb, but heavy, wrapped in indigo dashiki wave fabric through which I could feel sharp contours.

"From Laplace F."

She met Sergei through small, treasured items like this. Aminata, a Colloquium-mate, had introduced Shahina to the Digs. No digging was involved. Archaeologists, historians, some extreme sports fans took off in sasuits, rovers, dust-bikes out across the Mares in search of old space hardware. Lunar landers, rovers, construction bots, and solar sinterers from the early days of the settlement. Most prized was the dusty, dented detritus of the Apollos. They called this practical archaeology. I thought it barefaced looting but I could not say so to Shahina. Sergei financed it. He was some minor Vorontsov. One of the Five Dragons. I was still not disappointed when Shahina dropped him.

I turned the small precious thing over and over in my fingers.

"What is it?"

"History."

Terminal velocity in a pressurized lunar habitat is sixty kilometers per hour.

Callisto dreams.

E dreams in code, in shaped packets of electrons, as we all dream. All dreams are coded, and codes. AI dreams are not our dreams. Callisto dreams awake. E never sleeps, never needs to sleep. Callisto has difficulty understanding the human need for sleep, what it is, how we return from it the same as we entered; that we return from it at all. And Callisto dreams in er three separate manifestations: the mainframe, the probe, the blimp. I like to believe e shares dreams, like a family around the breakfast table in some café.

If Callisto's intelligence and emotions are genuine—some still believe they aren't and I have argued and will argue again their error with them—then so are er dreams. Marid translates them into a form I can comprehend. Callisto's dreaming is primarily auditory. Marid plays me a storming chatter of notes and clicks, titanic bass and infra bass swells and clusters of rushing triads at the very upper limit of my hearing. It sounds like chaos. It sounds like the throb of black holes, the drone of the cosmic microwave background, the slow tick of entropy towards dissolution and chaos but if you listen, if you really listen, if you go beyond the human instinct to analyze, to structure, the pareidolic need to sees rabbits in the Moon, faces on Mars, gods in the alignments of the stars, then a titanic music unfolds. Themes, harmonies—though by no harmonic laws we recognize—modes and variations, unfolding over a timescale longer than any human attention span. It is magnificent and beautiful and quite the eeriest thing I have ever heard. I drop into the dream-music and when I return, reeling, hard-of-breath and dazed, hours have passed.

I used to try to imagine what it must be like to dream constantly, to have this music rattling and burbling along the bottom of your consciousness like water over rocks. I understand now. The thing it must be like is imagination. That not-conscious but not-dreaming state of images, scenarios, illusions where we pursue potentials, alternatives, what-ifs. The imagination never closes, never quiets. It is the root of our humanity.

She got out of Aristarchus with three minutes of air to spare.

I'm all right, she said. *There's nothing wrong, nothing to see.* I came anyway, on the next express.

Three minutes, three hundred minutes.

But you could have died in there. How reluctantly I formed and spoke that word: *died.*

She was, as she said, all right. As she said, *if you didn't die, you were untouched.*

I hadn't heard from Shahina in three months. By heard from, I mean that in the old, Earthy sense—I hadn't seen, visited; been voice-called by her. I read her updates. Her posts and pictures and comments. I circled her social world with slow wingbeats but I was not of it. I could have called but it was a principle.

I must have read that she'd drifted away from the archaeologists, I must have seen the pictures of herself with her new friends, the explorers, leaning against each other, making gestures with their hands, pouting and posing and laughing. *Urbanisme*: I know that word, but I can only have learned it from Shahina's posts. I was working in a contract with Taiyang developing the interface for their new system of three AIs for Whitacre Goddard Bank; the ones—the legends said—that would be able to predict the future. The Suns expect work for their money; I remember long hard hours at the desk, digging deep, building layers, distilling out emotions from algorithms like botanicals in custom gin. There is no more tiring work than emotion work. I must have read Shahina's posts in a blur of exhaustion, taken them in at some level beneath analytic consciousness. I remember excitement. New friends, new group identity, new sport. Sport it was. Archaeology pretended to intellectual merit; urbanisme was adventure.

Her first exploration was to the old Mackenzie Metals habitat at Crisium, long abandoned since the Mackenzies moved their operations base to Crucible, the furnace-train that constantly circles the Moon, maintaining constant noon sun on its smelter-mirrors. By train then rover to Crisium, into sasuits and down into the abandoned tunnels. Afterwards, I watched all her videos. Headlamp beams lancing out through the passageways. Dust kicked up by booted feet. Lamps lighting up rooms and chambers and the mumble of audio commentary; we think this a mess hall; according to the maps, this is the old board room. Desks, furniture, graffiti. Screens, from the days before information was beamed on to the eyeball. Nothing organic: even then the Lunar Development Corporation's zaballeens recycled all carbon ferociously. Beams of light shooting upwards, bouncing from the walls of an old agriculture shaft, reflecting from the mirror array that once conveyed sunlight down to the stacks of aeroponics racks. Ovals of light overlapping on the gentle up-ramp of the main outlock. I watched with my heart in my throat, my hands to my mouth. I saw a thousand mistakes, ten thousand accidents, any of which could jam a valve, smash a helmet, gash a sasuit open. The Moon has a thousand ways to kill you: every Moon-child is taught that, the same hour that the chib is bonded to the eyeball and forever after you owe for the air you breathe, the water you drink, the carbon you consume, the data you process. I don't believe I drew breath until I saw the final image: the team shot beside the rover; faceless helmets inclined towards each other, sasuits smudged with dark moondust. Body shapes beneath the close-fitting suits, the appended name tags over the left shoulders were the only clues. Shahina was between two young men, her arms around their shoulders. I would have recognized her without the tag. Sunlight spangled from her helmet visor. I knew she was grinning.

Her second expedition was to Orientale. I studied there when I first came to the Moon. In those tunnels I worked and loved. In one of those small cabins I passed my Moonday, alone, knees pulled to my chest, hiding from all the friends and colleagues who wanted to take me out and splash my head with industrial vodka and proclaim me a true daughter of the Moon. Alone and weeping I rocked, terrified that I had made the wrong decision, knowing that it was now impossible to undo it. I could never go back to Earth again. My bones would sag and snap, my lungs fail, my heart flutter under a gravity my body had forgotten. I watched her stalk through the airless corridors, narrower than I remember; shine her light into the cubicles and labs, tighter than I remember. It seemed five minutes since I had lived there, yet I couldn't believe that I—that anyone—had lived there. I don't know what I would have done if her weaving beam had caught some discarded part of my past—vacuum-dried shorts, a glass, a cosmetics sachet. Ghosts of myself. It would have been equally strange for Shahina, I suppose: evidence of a time before she existed. If she could even recognize that debris as mine. I was glad when the video cut to the team hug at the end.

On her third expedition, the roof came in. Opening shot: Shahina and their friends at the station, the express pulling in behind them. They've printed matching tanktops: *Urbanisme: Aristarchus*. Train, then three hours by rover to the ruins at Aristarchus. Two hundred people died when a deep quake—the rarest and most dangerous of the many seisms that shake the Moon—popped the Corta Hélio maintenance base like a bubble. I watched this afterwards, understand. I still wanted to take the next train to Meridian and snatch my daughter up and whisk her away with me, safe, secure. If I had seen this as live feed, I would have spent every last bitsie on a Vorontsov moonship and still gone into debt for a century to haul her out.

Corta Hélio never brought the bodies back from Aristarchus. Too dangerous.

They had maps, AI guidance, satellite tracking, they knew that dead site like they knew their own skins; they went in safe, sane, and prepared but they still weren't expecting the temblor that brought down their main access tunnel. Ten meters of highly fragmented KREEP between them and the surface. They used their wit, they used their skill, they used their fit smart bodies. There was an old conduit shaft that carried power and coms from the surface to the habitat. It was five hundred meters, a vertical climb, through tangled cabling and smashed struts sharp as spears, camera, handholds, world shaking to the aftershocks. Shahina kept the camera running throughout. I knew the outcome but I watched with my hands over my mouth.

She made it to the rover with three minutes oxygen to spare. They all made it.

Three minutes, three hundred minutes, she said. To weaken my position, she brought two fellow Urbanistes to meet me. They were tall and languorous and moved beautifully. I felt small, I felt old, I felt obsolete. I felt awed by my daughter. She seemed a different species from me.

She messaged me privately on the train, familiar to familiar. She was getting out of urbanisme anyway. The boys were too up their own asses. The climb out of the dead habitat had taught her something about herself: she could move. Her body was strong and accurate. She liked to move. She had learned to love her physicality.

She was taking up parkour.

Why should a space probe have emotions? Why would e even need such things? In the early days of exploration, probes were no smarter than insects and they opened up whole new worlds inside the world we thought we knew. No smarter, and with even less emotional freight. They trundled, cold and heartless, across the hillsides of Mars, swung soulless and free from wonder over the methane seas of Titan.

My first answer is: why should an Artificial Intelligence not have emotions? But that is really not an answer, just a rhetorical device, so I follow it with this: since the 2076 Bamako Agreement, it is the right of every Artificial Intelligence to perceive and enjoy specific internal states which are analogous to emotions in human beings. To which you say: this is the Moon. No one has any rights. No rights, no civil law, only contracts between parties.

My second answer is: this exploration is part financed by subscription to live feeds, from within the atmosphere of Saturn. The old national space administrations learned their images from the surface of Mars were much better received when spiced with emotionality, even if that was added by a social media agent on Earth. Humans love emotionality. Make us *feel* something; then we understand. Give us the tiniest empathy with what it feels like to drive into the unimaginable wind shear of Hexagon, the north polar vortex. *What it is to be . . .* The essential human question.

And I'll have my third answer ready before your riposte: what is exploration? It is curiosity, the desire to know what is beyond those clouds; over that horizon. It is courage and caution, it is excitement and fear; it is the tension between risk and the desire for knowledge. A probe that knows emotion—its analogues of those emotions, for how can we ever really know what's in the head of another, be that bone or plastic—is better able to explore, to risk, to be cautious, to assess risk: to dare.

But it's my last answer that's in the end my first and only answer. Emotions are the nature of space probes, of express trains, of helium three extractors, and solar sinterers, of the orbital transfer tethers wheeling around the waist of our world. Emotions are an emergent property. You can no more make an Artificial Intelligence without emotions than you can a baby without tears, a daughter without curiosity. Why should an Artificial Intelligence have emotions, you asked? And I said, why not? But both of those are wrong. It's not a why question, or a because answer. Emotions are part of the universe.

She went up the side of Gagarin Prospekt in such great bounds, so fast, so agile I thought for a moment she was flying. From the park bench to the top of the printshop, printshop roof to ventilator pipe. Two heartbeats and she was crouching on the handrail of West 3rd, toes and fingers curled in their gloves, grinning down at me a dozen meters below. She had cut her hair to a bob so as not to interfere with her running, but Egyptian curls are not vanquished so easily. They fell around her face, lively and bobbing in lunar gravity. Then a shake and she sprang up again, outstretched, flying, one jump taking her to within reach of a lighting stanchion. She stretched, reached, grabbed, swung, somersaulted away to rebound from a balustrade onto the veranda of an apartment two levels higher. She stood like a little god, hands on hips. She looked up. The ten thousand lights of Orion Quadra shone above her, and higher than all of them, the sun line fading towards night.

She grabbed a corner of a roof truss, ran up the wall, and launched herself towards those higher lights.

And her pack mates, her follow *traceurs* flew with her. Like liquid, like animals, so fast and sleek and beautiful I found it almost alien. Human beings could not perform such wonders.

The invitation had been for the Colloquium Cotillion—its annual graduation when family and dearest of all Colloquium members are invited to a reception and dinner—but Shahina wanted me to see her run. It was all she talked of at the restaurant; moves and holds, stunts and technical wear, customized grip soles and whether it was more authentic to free run without familiar assistance. I understood one word in five but I saw the dark energy, the constrained passion, and I thought I had never seen her so young or so beautiful.

Of course I went to the run. I was the only parent. These young people, as tall and beautiful as any, didn't seem haughty or disdainful to me. These wiry, athletic boys, these dark-skinned muscular girls, restless and pacing or still and haunting, intensely focused on their world, their sport, their challenge. I was as invisible as a ghost, but, as the legends say, there are no ghosts on the Moon. Shahina, wire-thin but stronger than I had ever seen her before, in tights and the cropped, baggy T-shirt that was the fashion that season, foot and hand gloves, intent in conversation with two fellow *traceurs*. I could clearly see that they adored her. *Traceur*, that word, it was important, Shahina impressed on me. A name, an identity, a tribe. She had been free-running for six months now.

This was the pack's greatest challenge yet. All the way to the top of Orion Quadra, to touch the sun line, three kilometers up.

I saw her leap. My heart stopped as she flew out over the drop to bustling Gagarin Prospekt. She flew far, she flew true, she snatched a cable on a cross-quadra bridge and, a hundred meters above the ground, swung herself onto the crosswalk. She ran along the balustrade, balanced perfectly, as her *traceurs* swung up from beneath the bridge, dropping into position around her like an honor guard. Pedestrians, runners, strollers, workers going on-shift stared in amazement and I, craning my neck and ordering Marid to up the magnification on my lens, thought: don't you wish you were as hot and beautiful and sheerly magnificent as my daughter? Amazement and no small envy.

Up she flew, a blur of motion and speed, the pack racing with her but Shahina always a foot, a hand, a finger ahead of them. Marid focused, refocused, focused again, tighter and tighter as she climbed higher and higher. The race was as much horizontal as vertical: this was not climbing, Shahina had carefully lectured me at the banquet. This was parkour, and she ran ledges, overhanded along cables and danced on railings to find the best route up to the next level. Upward and upward. It was beautiful to watch. I had never been so afraid; I had never been so exhilarated.

Marid zoomed out for a moment to show me the true scale of the adventure and I gasped; the *traceurs* were flecks of movement on the towering walls of the world; brief absences in the patterns of light. Insects. Shahina has never known insects. My familiar lensed in again. They were above the inhabited levels now, even the mean shanties of the Bairro Alto where the up-and-out of Meridian society retreat: the old industrial and service levels, the first diggings from which Meridian grew downward, delving three kilometers deep. Here was the *traceurs*' playground; a world of handholds and surfaces and levels. A giant climbing frame. The race was on. I could not see Shahina's face when one of the boys passed her but I knew the expression that would be on it. I had seen those narrowed eyes, lips; that set of the jaw so many times in childhood and adolescence.

They were within touch of the sun.

Then Shahina jumped: too soon, too far, too short. Her gloved fingers missed the hold. And she fell.

Callisto dreams in other ways than sound. Marid has fractioned out all the millions of simultaneous streams of code that is machine dreaming and tagged them. Some are best experienced as sound—the oceanic symphony. Others only make sense—begin to make any kind of sense . . . visually. Marid feeds these to my lens.

I see colors. Stripes and bands of soft pastel color—there is an internal logic here, no clashing disharmonies of pink against red against orange. There is always a logic to dreaming. Motion: both I and the strips of color seem to be in motion, they stream past me and each other at various speeds—all I get is the sense that these bands of flowing color are immense. Beyond immense. Of planetary scale.

I said that in the refectory to Constantine, my colleague on the Callisto project. He deals with emergent emotional states in low-level intelligences. He's a Joe Moonbeam—a recent immigrant—so he still thinks in terms of animals and animal behavior—*like a family of kittens*, he compares them. I deal with the insecurities and identity issues of grand AI: *like adolescents*, I say. I looked at our refectory. A long barrel vault that discloses its original purpose as an access tunnel for the mining equipment which hacked the university out of Farside. I've seen sculptural bronze casts of terrestrial termite mounds: helices of tunnels and chambers dozens of meters tall, hundreds of meters across. I've spent my lunar life—almost all of Shahina's life—scuttling through those twining, claustrophobic tunnels. I try not to think of the termites, shriveling and burning in molten bronze. I thought of sherbet under the trees of Meridian's Orion Quadra, the face of the flying woman looking down on me, and I felt refectory, tunnels, university, Farside wrap themselves around me like bands of bronze.

Of planetary scale.

Callisto the probe will furl er light sail and enter orbit around Saturn. E will conduct orbital surveys for a month. Then Callisto the entry vehicle will detach, make er distancing burn and enter Saturn's upper atmosphere. E will plunge through the tropopause and use the uppermost deck of ammonia clouds to decelerate to 1800 kilometers per hour. One hundred and seventy kilometers below, at the second cloud deck, Callisto Explorer will drop heat shields and begin live streaming back through Callisto Orbiter. In the third cloud layer, one hundred and thirty kilometers below the second layer, the temperature averages 0 degrees C. Here Callisto Explorer will unfurl er balloon. Scoops will gather and inflate the bag, lasers will heat the gathered hydrogen for buoyancy. Ducted fans will deploy for maneuvering, but Callisto Explorer is a creature of the winds. We have designed er well, strongly, even beautifully. Er buoyancy bags are held inside a strong nanoweave shell; Callisto will cruise like a shark, ever moving, flying the eternal storms of Saturn.

I jabbered my insight to Constantine. He's used to my sudden seizures of understanding. We had been together a long time, as colleagues, as occasional amors, who may yet love again.

Those bands of color, furling and streaming, twining and hurtling, are differing layers and jet streams and storms of Saturn's atmosphere.

E is trying to imagine er future. And the music is the wind, the endless wind. A lone song in the endless roaring wind.

I saw my daughter fall from the edge of the sun line. I think I screamed. Every head on Gagarin Prospekt turned to me; then, as their familiars clued them in, to the sky.

No don't, don't look, don't watch, I yelled.

Acceleration under gravity on the surface of the Moon is 1.625 meters per second squared.

Mean atmospheric pressure inside lunar habitats is 1060 kilopascals, significantly higher than terrestrial norm.

Terminal velocity in a pressurized quadra is sixty kilometers per hour.

It takes four minutes to fall the height of Orion Quadra. Four minutes is time enough for a smart girl to save her life.

Impact at sixty kilometers and you have an eighty percent chance of dying. Impact at fifty kilometers per hour and you have an eighty percent chance of living.

She spread her arms and legs.

I could not take my eyes off her. Every part of my body and mind had stopped dead, vacuum-frozen.

Shahina presented as wide as cross section to the air as she could. Her hair streamed back, her T-shirt flapped like a flag. Her T-shirt might brake her to a survivable fifty kilometers per hour. Her fashionable baggy T-shirt might just save her life.

Still I couldn't look away. People were running, medical bots converging on the place she would hit the street. Still I couldn't move.

Four minutes is a long time to look at death.

She was low, so low, too low. The other *traceurs* were racing back down the walls of the world, dropping onto streets and walkways and escalators to try to race Shahina to the ground but this challenge she would always win.

I closed my eyes before the impact. Then I was running, pushing through the helpful people, shouting. *This is my daughter, my daughter!* The medical bots were first to arrive. Between their gleaming ceramic bodies I saw a dark spider broken on the street. I saw a hand move. I saw my daughter push herself up from the ground. Stagger to her feet. Then she fell forwards and the med bots caught her.

Nuur.

"What is it Callisto?" As you work with an AI, as er emotions firm and ground, as you learn er like you learn a child or an amor, you pick up nuances, overtones even in synthesized speech. My client was anxious.

My mission . . .

Callisto has learned the weight of the significant pause, the thing unsaid.

"Your mission."

Callisto Orbiter will remain in orbit under nuclear power until critical systems fail. I anticipate this will be a matter of centuries, based on the interaction of variables such as charged particles, Saturn's magnetic field, cosmic ray events. But at some point in the 25th century, give or take a few decades, Callisto Orbiter will die.

"Yes Callisto."

Callisto Explorer is scheduled for a three-year mission inside the cloud layers of Saturn, exploring meteorological and chemical features. My systems will certainly last longer than the mission schedule, but at some time in the near future my structural integrity will fail, I will lose buoyancy. I will fall. If I do not undergo complete disintegration, I will fall towards the liquid hydrogen layer under increasing pressure until my body is crushed. Nuur, I can feel that pressure. I can feel it squeezing me, breaking me, I can feel everything in me going flat and dark under it. I can feel the liquid hydrogen.

"That's what we call imagination, Callisto."

I can see my own death, Nuur.

This is the price of imagination. We foresee and feel our own deaths. We see the final drop, the last breath, the last close of the eyes, the final thought evaporating and beyond it nothing, for we can imagine nothing. It is no thought, no imagining, and though we know there can be no fear, no anything, in nothing, it terrifies us. We end. This is why imagination is what makes us human.

I'm afraid.

"It's the same for all of us, Callisto. I'm afraid too. We are all afraid. We would deal, barter, make any trade for it not to be so, but it must be. Everything ends. We can copy you forever, but every copy is an intelligence of itself . . . "

And it dies.

"Sorry Callisto."

No, I'm sorry for you. A pause that I have learned to interpret as a sigh. *How can we live this way?*

"Because there is no other way, Callisto."

She looked so small in the hospital bed.

Well don't stand there in the doorway, come in or don't come in.

I have always been a ditherer, hesitant to commit between one state and another, one world and another. I came to the Moon because my research, the drift of my career, made it inevitable. I howled with grief on my Moonday, because I could not tell my own will from dithering.

"How . . . "

It doesn't hurt at all really. They have these amazing painkillers. They should make the license public. Kids could print them out for parties. It's like I'm flying. Sorry. Bad joke. That's the painkillers. It kind of loosens things, breaks down boundaries. Nothing broken, nothing ruptured; quite a lot of heavy bruising.

I made space among the medical machinery and sat beside her. For a moment I saw her on the med-center bed as I saw her on Gagarin Prospekt, a broken spider, elongated and alien. She was born looking like every baby in human history: all the generation twos are. The differences only become apparent as they grow through years of lunar gravity. She grew tall, lean, layered with a different musculature aligned to her birth-world. Light as a wish. By age ten she was as tall as me. By twelve she was ten centimeters taller than me.

She hit the street and lived because she is a Moon-kid. I knew with utter certainty that if it had been me, falling from the top of the world, I would have died.

I took her hand. She winced.

Now that does hurt a bit.

"Please never . . . "

I can't promise that.

"No, I don't suppose you can."

The launch lasers at the VTO facility out at the L2 point have been firing for three days now. If I pulled on a sasuit and went to the surface and looked up I could see the brightest star in heaven, the reflection from Callisto's light sail. But I am not the kind of person who pulls on a sasuit and dashes up onto the surface. My daughter did that—would still do it—without a thought. I have never been that daring. This world frightens me, and I can have no other.

Callisto will shine there for several months before VTO shuts down the lasers and e sails out by sunlight alone to er missions at Saturn. Light sails are effective but slow. Callisto sleeps. In er sleep, e dreams. In those dreams, I know, will be the tang and sting of mortality. All these wonders; er ecstatic plunge through Saturn's cloud layers, er adventures flying alone and beautiful through the eternal storms, seeing things no human can ever see; all these will be once and once only, and all the more sweet before they vanish forever. Will the knowledge that everything is ephemeral make Callisto seek out stronger, more vivid experiences to beam back to er subscribers? I think so but that was not the reason I worked the knowledge of mortality into Callisto's emotional matrix. I did it because e could not be fully intelligent without it.

Before the project uploaded Callisto to the probes, I believe I came to love er as fully as I have any human. A copy of er still remains on the university mainframe, always will. I can wake er up at any time to talk, share, joke. I won't. It would be talking to the dead, it would be ghosts and the Moon allows no ghosts.

Shahina fell three kilometers and walked away. She's famous. A celebrity. She's sufficiently sanguine to work it while it's warm: go to the parties, do the interviews, join the social circles. It won't last. She can't wait to be able to go running again. What more can the Moon do to her? I can't stop her, I won't watch her. A mother should only have to watch her daughter fall once.

Callisto falls outward from our little clutch of two worlds, so small in the scheme of things. It will take er two years to reach Saturn. Humans can't go there. The universe is hard on us; these are not our worlds. Not even Shahina and her cohort, or even the generation three growing up high and strange in our underground cities, could go there. Whatever makes it from these worlds to the stars, won't be us. Can't be us. But I like to think I sent something human out there.

Burn bright, little star. Tonight I catch the train to Meridian where Shahina has invited me to a celebrity party. I'll hate the party. I'm as fearful of it as I am the surface; I'll cling to the wall with my nonalcoholic drink and watch the society people and watch my beautiful, alien daughter move among them.

Originally published in *Meeting Infinity,* edited by Jonathan Strahan.

ABOUT THE AUTHOR

Ian McDonald is a SFF writer living in Northern Ireland, just outside Belfast, by the sea. He's a multiple-ward winning writer, and his most recent writings are *Luna: New Moon* and *Luna: Wolf Moon* (Tor, Gollancz) and novella *Time was,* from Tor.com. Forthcoming is *Luna: Moon Rising.*

Endless Forms Most Horrible: Parasites and SF

JULIE NOVAKOVA

> "*Certain wasp-like insects, which construct in the corners of the verandahs clay cells for their larvae, are very numerous in the neighbourhood of Rio. These cells they stuff full of half-dead spiders and caterpillars, which they seem wonderfully to know how to sting to that degree as to leave them paralysed but alive, until their eggs are hatched; and the larvae feed on the horrid mass of powerless, half-killed victims—a sight which has been described by an enthusiastic naturalist as curious and pleasing!*"
>
> —Charles Darwin, *The Voyage of The Beagle* (Chapter II)

He's running for his life—but eventually his struggle ends in vain. The alien descends on him and delivers her sting, and then another. He finds himself paralyzed after the first, so the second one can be delivered precisely into his brain. He cannot move as the sharp tip penetrates his head. Afterwards, he begins to feel contented, lethargic. The alien leads him to her lair and lays a single egg on his belly. He watches helpless as it hatches and the larva burrows into him. He feels it gnawing through his insides, but can't do anything about it. He's still alive for most of the time; the larva knows to leave the most vital organs for last.

It sounds like a scene from some gory SF, doesn't it? Except this kind of thing happens quite normally in the real world—only the alien is a parasitoid wasp, and its victim a cockroach.

The real Alien

Especially among insects and most prominently wasps, there are countless parasitoid species: many that need a single host for a part of their lifetimes and then discard it dead. Some live *on* their hosts, some *inside* them; there are situations where different parasitoid species can meet in a single host, or even parasitoids using *other parasitoids* as their hosts. Such scenarios are common in nature and would be interesting to explore in the realm of science fiction, but "simple" parasitoid occurrences are most frequent in the genre, the best known being the cult franchise *Alien*. You have likely felt the horror when the almost-mature xenomorph burst from Gilbert Kane's chest, killing him.

What are the chances we'd meet a parasitoid among alien life? I'd say that if we encounter a complex biosphere, the odds are pretty high, practically certain. On Earth, parasitic—including parasitoid—life strategies have evolved countless times independently in many lineages, and nearly half of all described species are parasites. But don't worry: the odds of encountering a xenomorph seem next-to-nothing, since most parasites have coevolved with their hosts for a long time and are adapted only to a limited range of hosts, frequently a single species.

In any case, *Alien* didn't come up with anything entirely new in the genre. Its story, atmosphere, suspense, and visuals have just made it a cult classic. But science fiction, fantasy and horror have contained the theme of parasites from the very beginning, even from their folklore and mythical roots. (Although, to be fair, vampires that don't kill their victims aren't technically parasites in the narrow sense but micropredators—like mosquitoes—and those who kill are simply predators.)

Parasites can be found in Victorian novels (e.g. *Dracula* by Bram Stoker and *The Beetle* by Richard Marsh, both published in 1897). Those readers knew about parasites quite well and both feared and loathed them. And newer works? We can see a lot of parasitic life strategies in them. Perhaps surprisingly, brood parasitism—common not just in cuckoos, honeyguides, cowbirds, and some other bird species, but also in other lineages of life, seems rather rare in modern speculative fiction. John Wyndham's SF novel *The Midwich Cuckoos* is a prime example, but we actually see a lot of this parasitic strategy in myths and legends. Just think of elves stealing human babies and replacing them with their own kin.

Pulp and Golden Age SF seems rife with parasites of various kinds. The space being Ixtl in A. E. van Vogt's *The Voyage of The Space Beagle* is a parasitoid, laying eggs into the bellies of several crew members to eat them from the inside. Heinlein's *The Puppet Masters* introduce mind-controlling sluglike creatures who attempt to take over humanity, albeit with somewhat unclear strategy as what to do next or how their plan maximizes their fitness. But that's the trouble with SF parasites that possess intelligence: they tend not to reach the success, or the horror effect, of their less endowed cousins.

In Cronenberg's movie *Shivers* (1975), a parasite engineered by a mad scientist isn't intelligent, or at least doesn't seem so. It increases its hosts' sexual desire to the point where they become complete slaves to it. The parasite is mostly—though not solely—transmitted during sex. A similar strategy is suspected to be used by a number of real parasites, but there is surprisingly little solid evidence for it, perhaps because there are many host behavioral defenses to be overcome (such as "don't mate with someone who seems sick"). Even if observed, it might be just because a sick host, uncertain of their future reproductive prospects, attempts to go "all in" in the game of reproduction.

Some parasites, though, manage to make their host attractive . . . even if it's already dead. The parasitic fungus *Entomophthora muscae* first controls its host, a house fly, so that it flies to a high point and spreads its wings and legs so that the spores of the fungus that has grown through its entire body can be easily caught by wind and infect other flies. But that's not all: Infected (and dead) female flies become attractive for male flies, who can become infected by attempting to mate with the cadaver. Sounds gross? It certainly does; but "irresistible corpses" may be difficult to pull off in any fiction.

Mind control and body-snatchers

But what draws perhaps more attention and fear than such gory images is exactly the issue of mind-controlling parasites. After all, the idea of something or someone else seizing control of our selves seems appalling at least to most people. Be it the above-mentioned examples, Goa'uld in *Stargate*, Ceti eels and unnamed "parasitic beings" in *Star Trek*, Bezoar in *Buffy The Vampire Slayer*, headcrabs in *Half-Life*, they terrify us if executed well. Yet in reality, we are very much "the sum of our parts" consisting also of organisms other than human. The myriad of microorganisms—various protists, bacteria, archaea, viruses that are living inside our bodies, many of them practically indispensable for us, all affect not just our physical health, but also our mental states. Research on this so-called microbiome is still quite young, but there are numerous indications that the composition of our gut microbiome is linked to mood and behavior, especially stress response. On the other hand, we must be careful to correctly determine the cause and effect there. It's likely that our gut microbiome influences our moods, but also that our behavioral patterns impact the composition of microbes in our gut (because of our eating, exercising, and other habits). Which direction is the major one in this two-way relationship? That remains to be investigated more in-depth.

But most of the organisms in our gut are either commensals, or mutualists. They either don't do much good or bad for us and basically just consume the scraps that we don't want anymore, or they have a positive effect on our health. In truth, you'd never find a perfect commensal as their presence always has *some* effect and even mutualists can "turn bad" under special circumstances, but we can generalize and say that their presence is neutral or good. Our bodies are used to them and need many of them. We don't think of their influence over our mood and behavior as manipulation. But what about real parasites?

There are plenty of real-world examples of host manipulation. For instance, the rabies virus increases migratory behavior and aggressiveness in infected animals, increasing the chances for its long-distance transmission (by the way, outbreaks may have paved the way for werewolf trials and legends). The liver fluke *Dicrocoelium dendriticum* makes its second intermediate host, an ant, climb a grass blade and hang from it on its mandibles, so that the definitive host—a ruminant—can eat it. Caterpillars infected with baculoviruses seek high places in trees so that virions released from their dead bodies can reach more new victims. Hairworm-infected crickets jump into water when the parasite is mature, and drown while the worm crawls out of their bodies and happily swims away. The parasitic crustacean *Sacculina* (used fictitiously in Philip Fracassi's horror novella of the same name) not only castrates its crab hosts, but makes them take care of the spreading of its own progeny. Malaria-infected mosquitoes carrying infectious stages of the protozoan are more attracted to humans and tend to bite more people (though in this case, the parasite more likely co-opted the sickness response of the host rather than manipulating it outright).

Perhaps most famously, the malaria-related protozoan *Toxoplasma gondii* manipulates its intermediate hosts—typically rodents—to become easier prey to cats. They exhibit less fear (and cease to be afraid of cat odor, even become fatally attracted to it), are more active, and react more slowly. Several studies suggest that infected humans are more likely to fall prey to . . . cars. Slower reaction times and more risking tendencies are among the commonly observed effects in both rodents and humans, who are mostly "dead ends" for *T. gondii* these days. But how does the parasite achieve this? It seems that the protozoan influences its hosts' dopamine metabolism and thus behavior. *Toxoplasma*-infected individuals also display higher testosterone levels—decreasing their immune response and shifting behavior toward more risk-seeking and aggression (in male subjects) at once.

If more zombie stories were inspired by these real-world parasites, perhaps there would be much more variety to them. And indeed, there are examples of brilliantly executed stories using such themes: George R. R. Martin's *Men of Greywater Station* uses the trope of a parasitic fungus—except in the story, it has intelligence and agency, and manages to brilliantly manipulate not just its victims, but also the humans it hasn't infected yet. M. R. Carey's acclaimed novel *The Girl with All The Gifts* even uses a real fungal parasite, *Ophiocordyceps unilateralis* (which infects and "zombifies" insects in reality), as the source of an unusual zombie outbreak.

Note, however, that most behavior-manipulating parasites have more complex life cycles with at least one intermediate host, sometimes many of them and that's something we don't often see in science fiction. This trope might prove more interesting yet.

Parasites: loathed but indispensable . . . and wonderful

It might seem that parasites are horrible creatures that should be exterminated, but nothing can be further from the truth! Even if we set aside the ethical issues of causing a species' extinction, even though that species is considered harmful, many food webs are kept in delicate balance by some key species! Parasites often represent this linchpin, for example, by keeping a predator population in check and preventing it from growing too much, eliminating its prey and causing a whole domino effect in a given ecosystem. Sometimes, if we recognize the key role of a parasite, we can use it to limit populations of invasive species in an environment where the species was introduced without this natural regulation. It doesn't always work, but for example the parasitoid wasp *Trissolcus basalis* has proven successful in many regions where its host, the southern green stink bug, previously wreaked havoc on crops.

Still, this probably wouldn't make you willingly swallow a parasite, right? Despite that, there are reasons why you might want to do just that. If you have allergies or certain autoimmune disorders, exposure to parasites can actually alleviate your trouble. A parasitic worm that infects pigs, *Trichuris suis*, weakens the symptoms of Crohn's disease (probably by altering the gut microbiome) and presents no significant danger for humans. This kind of helminthic therapy is also used for other inflammatory gut diseases, and we may one day treat and try to prevent allergies with parasite-derived proteins. These trends have already made their way into science fiction: Mira Grant's Parasitology series uses a similar premise, in this case an engineered tapeworm enhancing the human immune system and other functions, for its SF-horror plot.

In terms of mood and behavior alteration, parasites might also be utilized deliberately. A slightly ironic docufiction article on *The Verge* recently explored the idea of using *T. gondii* voluntarily in the competitive, aggressive environment of Silicon Valley. Another instance where *T. gondii* occurred as a remedy of sorts was a mention in Peter Watts' novel *Echopraxia*. In reality, people are talking about changing not just their health but also their behavioral patterns through microbiome fecal transplants, and though the science is quite new, there will undoubtedly be many amateurs and biohackers experimenting with such new treatments . . . and a more than fertile ground for science fiction authors.

We tend to be horrified and disgusted by parasites and some of us wish to eliminate them completely. But in many ways, we depend on them. Food webs can hinge on them and they present an important evolutionary force. They might even offer avenues into medical research. Moreover, they are simply too interesting.

We still seek to understand the arms race they engage in with their hosts' immunity; how they manipulate hosts' behavior, both indirectly and directly. From producing neurotransmitters to utilizing symbiotic viruses. We have yet to learn the extent of the vital role they play in Earth's biosphere. It is presumed that the majority of species on Earth are or can facultatively become parasitic. Some are deadly; some effect their death toll only through minute changes in each host, outright killing none; some are evolving into helpful mutualists.

If you want to understand ecology and evolution, you can never leave out parasites. Thinking about them this way, as incredible and all-pervading creatures, you can perhaps finally understand the sentiment of Ash from Alien, saying with awe: "You still don't understand what you're dealing with, do you? The perfect organism. Its structural perfection is matched only by its hostility."

Note/disclaimer: The author works in the department led by Professor Jaroslav Flegr, who is among the leading researchers on *Toxoplasma gondii*'s behavioral effects in humans (though the author doesn't work on this topic herself). If you're interested in this research or helping science in general by participating in various (mostly online) studies, please consider joining the Lab Bunnies community at labbunnies.eu.

ABOUT THE AUTHOR

Julie Novakova is a Czech author and translator of science fiction, fantasy and detective stories. She has published short fiction in *Clarkesworld, Asimov's, Analog,* and other magazines and anthologies, and her translations of other authors' work appeared in *Tor.com, Strange Horizons,* and *F&SF.* Her work in Czech includes seven novels, one anthology (*Terra Nullius*), and over thirty short stories and novelettes. Some of her works have been also translated into Chinese, Romanian, Estonian, German and Filipino. She received the Encouragement Award of the European science fiction and fantasy society in 2013, the Aeronautilus award for the best Czech short story of 2014 and 2015, and for the best novel of 2015. Julie is an evolutionary biologist by study and also takes a keen interest in planetary science.

First Contact, Fantasy, and Cooperation: A Conversation with Steven Erikson

CHRIS URIE

Humanity has unconsciously defined itself as the lone intelligence in the universe. From our attitudes toward other species, to our own sometimes overblown sense of self-importance. For all intents and purposes, many of us believe that the universe revolves around us—until it doesn't.

Steven Erikson's new novel *Rejoice, A Knife to the Heart* tackles a question that has wracked the brains of many authors before: What happens when we discover that we aren't the all-powerful intelligence in the universe? Science fiction author Samantha August is abducted by aliens in broad daylight. In an instant, the entire planet knows that we aren't alone. Not only do the aliens abduct one of the planet's best loved authors to be their ambassador, but they start imposing their will worldwide, to help humanity save themselves from an apocalypse of their own making.

Steve Erikson is the *New York Times* and *Sunday Times* bestselling author of the epic fantasy series, *The Malazan Book of the Fallen.* He's also written numerous short stories and science fiction novels. His newest novel is *Rejoice, A Knife to the Heart.* It'll be available from Promontory Press on October 16th.

What first got you interested in writing?

I had early ambitions to be a comic book illustrator, but this was back in the day before anything digital existed, and it turned out to be a lot of work. Too much work. Since even my drawing had a narrative bent, I guess I naturally transitioned over to using just words.

Having written both fantasy and science fiction novels, which genre do you feel most at home working in?

That's changing, to be honest. It was so relaxing writing a basically mimetic novel. In a way, it brought me back to my short story writing origins in creative writing programs.

I still enjoy writing fantasy, but it's a much harder genre, to be honest. There are structural and stylistic impositions that simply aren't there with a mimetic novel. *Rejoice* was much closer to my natural style of speaking, writing, rhythm, and composition. Am I prevaricating here? Possibly.

If you had to choose one science fiction author to act as the communication conduit between humans and an alien race, who would you choose?

Were she still alive, Ursula K. Le Guin. Now, maybe Kim Stanley Robinson or Robert Sawyer.

Your novel struck me as somewhat subversive. It toys with some of the familiar alien invasion tropes but quickly flips them on their head. What inspired you to tackle an alien invasion story?

The subject has been of long interest to me, and I've read scads of First Contact novels, some brilliant, some not so much. Basically, *Rejoice* is a thought experiment. I think many First Contact novels carry with them some dubious assumptions, particularly when it comes to what's out there (who's out there) and how they might proceed to initiate and engage in contact with our species. I felt the desire to upend some of those assumptions, although I would humbly suggest that the subversive elements are less about alien tropes than about human society and modern civilization.

But to stay with your question, as part of my thought experiment I needed to establish some basic premises:

1. Alien species capable of traveling between stars are probably post-scarcity (there is growing evidence that space is rife with resources).
2. Alien species will approach us from a position that dispenses with (or ignores) our hierarchical, nationalistic obsessions.
3. Proper, full, First Contact must engage with all members of our species, not just government agencies or any other choke points (said agencies being the self-proclaimed gatekeepers to information would be counterproductive to initiating a fundamental, existential shift in the thinking our species engages in, said shift being utterly necessary to our being welcomed into a galactic community)
4. The only effective First Contact will involve both carrot and stick.
5. Secrecy is anathema: what changes occur must occur to each and every one of us, and those among our species obsessed with secrecy are in fact obsessed with power and domination: that attitude needs humbling.

The most interesting parts of your novel aren't the alien invaders, it's humanity's reactions to the limitations placed on the planet and society. What made you decide to have the aliens impose these particular limitations?

If there is a barrier to contact, it's to do with our attitudes, our ways of engaging in those aspects of human behavior we assume to be innate, sociobiological even: competition over cooperation, aggression over agreement, territoriality over the common, hierarchy over egalitarianism, and so on. Most people will assert the dominance of such self-serving traits via a recursive, oxymoronic, and self-justifying melange of capitalist ethos, individualism, even genetics, which strikes me as misplaced emphasis—humanity achieves civilization through cooperation, and when cooperation breaks down, so does civilization. As any archaeologist will tell you. We acquire civilization, societal peace, and well-being in counterpoint to our worse tendencies, those negative impulses that break down community or work to curtail it.

Accordingly, we need a shift in our thinking (and yes, it would present the most profound existential crisis our species has ever experienced) and, thus far it seems, we can't do it on our own. Hence the external imposition on our most cherished behaviors of unfettered expansion and rapacious self-expression.

Your novel, like many great science fiction novels, tackles a number of "what if" scenarios. For example: What if aliens prevented humans from decimating our environmental resources. What is one scenario you would have liked to include in your novel but didn't quite have the chance?

Hmm, how about an *explicit* slap of reason, delivered to everyone?

Rejoice juggles a more personal story of Samantha August's abduction with a worldwide global catastrophe as seen through numerous other characters. Did you find it difficult to keep the story grounded as you shifted perspective all around the world?

Not at all. Samantha's story needed a counterpoint, a more tactile sense of what people were experiencing on the planet's surface. If anything, the challenge was in keeping the number of other stories manageable—I could easily have added another ten or so new character points-of-view. Instead, I tried for a representative selection that tackled the experience from various levels, from the kid on the street to the working woman and man to religious figures to politicians to scientists and so on. That also served in varying the voices used.

How did you go about creating the various POV characters around the world?

The key for me was in covering as much of the planet as possible: not just one country or one culture.

Is Samantha August a wholly unique creation or an amalgam of science fiction authors throughout history?

She's an amalgam of Ursula K.Le Guin and maybe Margaret Atwood: Le Guin for her "social" SF approach and Atwood for her edginess. When I conjured up a physical image of her in my head, it was Meryl Streep (!!!).

Your novel is struck through with some clever commentary on humanity, politics, and the environment. Do you believe science fiction has the power to change minds or at the very least encourage someone to think differently?

It'd be nice to think so, but only in the sense of all fiction offering to a reader that potential for a shift in perspective. Historically, do we really see any efficacy in SF? Was Orwell's *1984* sufficient warning against totalitarianism? Was Huxley's *Brave New World* a heeded warning on the dangers of collective somnolence? These sonorous bells ring on and on, don't they? Who knows, maybe only dogs hear them.

What projects are you working on next?

I am working on the new trilogy set in the Malazan world (the epic fantasy series).

Would you like to be abducted by aliens? If so, which kind?

My bags are packed. Which kind? The kind that I think are probably out there.

ABOUT THE AUTHOR

Chris Urie is a writer and editor from Ocean City, NJ. He has written and published everything from city food guide articles to critical essays on video game level design. He currently lives in Philadelphia with an ever expanding collection of books and a small black rabbit that has an attitude problem.

Another Word: In Praise of Taking it Slow

SARAH PINSKER

I'm here to talk to you about the Slow Fiction Movement. Okay, that's not a thing, but it should be. Much as slow food encompasses every aspect of production, culminating with consumption, the idea of slow fiction speaks to every stage of a story's life cycle.

I should clarify that I'm not talking about drafting speed, nor productivity. Go about your initial drafting at whatever pace works for you. Bradbury believed in writing the first draft with gusto, but didn't discourage editing after that energetic outpouring of prose. His "don't be afraid to explore the attic" is closer to what I'm getting at; you never reach the attic if you don't leave enough time to get past the ground floor.

No, I'm here to speak for any slowdown that helps you make your story the best story it can be, whether that's at the idea phase or the first draft, or sometime after that initial draft has made it to the page, after you've celebrated the successful translation of inspiration to prose, when you're still excited about what you've accomplished.

When writing to a theme or prompt, it's often said that you should discard the first idea that comes to mind. The first is superficial, the obvious thing, a story that is writable but not necessarily worth writing. Give the prompt time to rattle around with everything else in your head and you may come up with something far better. The same goes for non-prompted stories: your first idea, as shiny as it is, is often the easy version. Ted Chiang has said in interviews that he plays with a concept for a long time before even starting to draft; the ideas that stick with him are the ones he takes the time to write. Connie Willis has advised her Clarion students to think of their stories just before they go to bed, so the subconscious gets a bite at it.

Some stories simply need more time. The ideas need breathing room, or the author needs time to develop the skills to write it. I took my novelette "Wind Will Rove" to the Sycamore Hill peer workshop in 2015, then put it aside for a year before revising it. The advice at the workshop was encouraging and thoughtful, but I knew I wasn't ready to do the work necessary to transform a good draft into the story I thought it could be. I thought about it during that time, and how to make the changes, all without touching the document again until I thought I was ready.

Learn to recognize the stories you aren't ready to write yet. Incubate them and write other things. I asked Nebula and World Fantasy Award winner Alyssa Wong about this, and she said, "Sometimes a story isn't done until it is. And sometimes, you have to grow into the kind of writer who can write the story you need to tell, and that can take a long time. 'Hungry Daughters of Starving Mothers' took three years for me to figure out; I've been working on another since 2013, and I still haven't cracked it. And that's okay. I'm patient, because I'd rather tell the story as it needs to be told, rather than in a form that I'm not satisfied with (I've done that too). I think it's natural to worry about whether or not you're writing fast enough. But it's also important to be proud of your work, and I only send out a story when I know I can be proud of it."

Seanan McGuire wrote a series of tweets recently in which she said that, though she's a prolific author, "what sometimes seems to come as a surprise is the part where not every book can be written the second I think of it. Some books require me to do other things first. They need me to get BETTER."

Think of the personal satisfaction you'll feel completing a story that went beyond your initial idea to ask the next question, and the next, to probe edges, to delve deeper. The story you had time to read out loud, to edit not just for spelling errors but for rhythm, for language, for lyrical truth. The story with the first line that you found after writing the last line and realizing you could cut the first two paragraphs entirely. The story with the last sentence that makes you weep for its perfection.

In a 2016 interview with Meghan McCarron, Ted Chiang said, "As for advice to slow writers, I'd say that writing is not a race. This isn't a situation where only the most prolific writers get an audience; publish your story when you're ready, and it will find readers."

The temptation is there. A story out the door is a potential sale. Everyone wants to check off the bingo square that says "three professional sales," and "ten professional sales," etc. Each sale is its own rush, as is publication day, and slow fiction means those come less often. Still, there's something to be said for fewer, better stories.

We all wind up against immovable dates. Deadlines abound, and it's easy to wind up in the position of constantly writing up to them. They're everywhere: magazines with narrow windows, themed anthologies with open submissions, solicited stories I've agreed to write only to have the deadline settle its weighty body up against my subconscious.

"It's okay," I console myself. "You write clean first drafts."

I remind myself of Heinlein's rules, which I mostly agree with except for "you must refrain from rewriting," and of Bradbury's, which I prefer. I hit my word count, do an editing pass, and send it out the door, and a week later (if I'm lucky) or when the magazine comes out (if I'm not) I realize what I could have done with the story given more time.

My goal is to make those rushed stories the exception, rather than the rule. I've come around to the theory that those situations come up and need to be handled, but most stories are better for a little aging. (First draft essay simile: every story is better for a little aging, like a fine wine. Second draft essay: Wine is a boring comparison. Look up the effect of aging on meat. Is that a better comparison? Third draft: Or a stout! How many people even know you can age a stout? They develop nuances of flavor that blah blah blah . . .) Michael R. Underwood carried my simile forward, pointing out that there's a difference between folding herbs into a recipe and adding them in after it's cooked.

No, as long as I'm looking to classic SF writers for inspiration, I think I'm better off with Ursula K. Le Guin (when am I not?). On her website's FAQ, she answered the question "Do you revise many times?" with "As many times as necessary. With one story or novel, this may be five false starts and six or eight or ten full rewrites, beginning to end. With the next, it may mean just going back through it and over it fiddling details until I think it's as good as I can get it."

Or I can go with Sturgeon's "ask the next question." That's what my first-draft-and-out-the-door stories lack. A first draft has all the shine of the original inspiration, if I'm lucky enough to have removed it from my head intact, but it's often superficial. It has good bones, some turns of phrase I'm pleased with, characters and structure that carried me through. And yet it often lacks depth. The "why" or the "and then" to the "what if?"

A story I've finished without rush has time to go to one of my critique partners. Every story that I've put in front of other readers before sending it out is better for the extra travel. A beta reader is not in my head, and thus can only rely on what they see in front of them. They can answer the question of whether the idea survived the trip to the page far better than I can. An editor told me he can always tell which stories were sent out half-baked, and which were seen by beta readers.

We all miss things. We bring our own baggage, our own background. Things that seem obvious to us are not necessarily obvious to others, or vice versa. You described the people who ride the bus, but what about the driver? Problems I didn't foresee, contradictory actions, sensitivity reads. Think of all the pain you can save both yourself and your readers if you give yourself a chance to notice the stereotype you accidentally reinforced. You didn't mean to do it. You thought the metaphor was a clever one.

More than that. A week later, two weeks later, I'll be out for a run, and realize that a character should do THIS instead of THAT, or I should add a line about so and so. It's sometimes possible to do this in copy edits, but why risk it? Give yourself a chance to think about the story, but also not to think about it. To let it sit in the back of your brain instead of the front.

There's a difference between aging a story and sitting on a story. I'm not advocating holding onto it until your topical story becomes obsolete, or your deadline flatlines. I'm advocating letting it become a thing of craft instead of solely inspiration. A chance to level up. A collaboration between current you and future you.

Welcome to the Slow Fiction Movement.

ABOUT THE AUTHOR

Sarah Pinsker is the author of the Nebula winning novelette, "Our Lady of the Open Road" and the Theodore Sturgeon Award winning novelette, "In Joy, Knowing the Abyss Behind." Her stories have appeared in *Asimov's, Strange Horizons, Fantasy & Science Fiction, Lightspeed,* and *Uncanny,* among others, as well as numerous anthologies, and have been nominated for the Nebula, Hugo, Sturgeon, Locus, and Eugie Foster awards. Her first collection, *Sooner or Later Everything Falls Into the Sea: Stories* will be published by Small Beer Press in March 2019, followed by a novel, *Song For A New Day,* September 2019 from Ace/Berkley. She lives with her wife and dog in Baltimore, Maryland.

Editor's Desk: After the Dirty Dozen

NEIL CLARKE

It looks like October has swung back around already. That means *Clarkesworld* has turned twelve and is now in its thirteenth year. Good thing we're not superstitious! However, it occurs to me that I'm a bit overdue on another, "where we're going" editorials, so this seems like a good time to jump in and do that.

Six years—or half the life of the magazine—ago, I added reprints to each issue as a way of saying "thank you" for the kindness readers showed my family and I after my heart attack. Gardner Dozois was brought in as Reprint Editor and he handled that side of the house until his passing earlier this year. Since then, I've been selecting the reprints and giving some thought to their future place in *Clarkesworld*.

At any given time, we have a specific goal that new subscriptions or Patreon pledges are put towards. In the past, this has included things like more stories, an equipment budget for the podcast, pay raises for staff, etc.. The new goal is to begin converting those reprints to slots for more original fiction. Given the significant difference in costs, this will slowly fade in as the number of supporters increases. Unless everyone manages to surprise me, it will be some time before we're able to replace both reprints with originals, therefore I've broken it into chunks. The first target converts one reprint to an original in every other issue.

The reason for moving in this direction is simple. Original fiction is the heart of *Clarkesworld*. The more space we have for it, the more flexibility we have in what we can publish. You might have noticed that we quietly experimented with a few novellas in the past year. We'd like to be able to up our word count limits and do that more often. New—and different—voices are also important to us. Being able to take more stories from open submissions is a very big positive in our eyes. We never solicit original fiction, so this actually creates more opportunities for us to publish new authors.

But why remove reprints when you can just add more stories?

- Moving money from the reprint budget to the original fiction budget allows us to incorporate these changes much more quickly.
- Increasing our overall page count would have significant cost ramifications on the print edition.
- I have a second magazine, *Forever*, that is entirely focused on reprints and might be able to grow to include what is displaced from here. *Forever* didn't exist when the reprints were first introduced. If it did, I probably would have done things differently.

While we're working towards that goal, a few other projects will continue to bubble in the background. The biggest of these is somewhat timely, given this month's anniversary, so I'll announce it slightly ahead of schedule.

Clarkesworld was originally launched as a companion magazine to Clarkesworld Books, an online genre bookstore I ran for several years. The bookstore closed about a year later, but I found that I couldn't give up the magazine. That's why we're still here. If all goes as planned, a Kickstarter campaign will be launched later this month to reboot Clarkesworld Books as a translation-focused, short story-oriented, science fiction imprint of Wyrm Publishing. This imprint will allow us to build on the success we've had with our Chinese authors and create additional opportunities for authors from other countries. Specifically, the campaign will help fund our first collection, *A Hundred Ghosts Parade Tonight and Other Stories* by Xia Jia.

Xia Jia is a name that should be familiar to *Clarkesworld* readers. Over the years, we've published several of her stories and I'm not ashamed to admit that I'm a big fan of her work. I couldn't be more pleased to have her first English language collection—which will include several previously untranslated stories—as Clarkesworld Books' first title. If we hit stretch goals, we might even see another project announced.

I hope that some of you will consider supporting it when the campaign launches.

• • •

It wouldn't be right to end this month's anniversary issue editorial without giving a big thank you to everyone: staff, authors, artists, readers, listeners . . . this place doesn't exist without you and I'm so grateful for every day it does.

All the best,

-Neil

ABOUT THE AUTHOR

Neil Clarke is the editor of *Clarkesworld Magazine, Forever Magazine,* and *The SFWA Bulletin;* owner of Wyrm Publishing; and a six-time Hugo Award Nominee for Best Editor (short form). His anthologies include *Upgraded, Galactic Empires, More Human Than Human, The Final Frontier,* and the Best Science Fiction of the Years series. His next anthology is *Not One of Us*, which will be published in November by Night Shade Books. He currently lives in NJ with his wife and two children.

Cover Art: Postcards from Asia: The Floodplain

PAT PRESLEY

Pat Presley was born in the oldest part of Bangkok, The Rattanakosin Island, where he grew up in what he believed to be a haunted house full of snakes, trees, and ancient relics his grand-uncle collected. Besides attending an old French missionary school, he learned from watching. When it was the time to further his education he hoped to become a doctor just to make a lot of money, but then decided he best be an idealistic architect. Neither one panned out, so he stopped making plans and relearned everything from scratch. Pat went back to drawing late into the night and remembered how great it was to be a kid who gets to stay up way past his bedtime.

Although some people wonder about his age, he was old enough to see Star Wars in the theater.

28051127R00093

Made in the USA
Columbia, SC
08 October 2018